THE SCAPEGOAT

T H E

FARRAR, STRAUS AND GIROUX | NEW YORK

SCAPEGOAT

SARA DAVIS

Farrar, Straus and Giroux
120 Broadway, New York 10271

Library of Congress Cataloging-in-Publication Data
Names: Davis, Sara, 1985– author.
Title: The scapegoat : a novel / Sara Davis.
Description: First edition. | New York : Farrar, Straus and Giroux, 2021.
Identifiers: LCCN 2020046535 | ISBN 9780374181451 (hardcover)
Subjects: GSAFD: Mystery fiction.
Classification: LCC PS3604.A9757 S33 2021 | DDC 813/.6—dc23
LC record available at https://lccn.loc.gov/2020046535

Designed by Abby Kagan

Our books may be purchased in bulk for promotional, educational, or business
use. Please contact your local bookseller or the Macmillan Corporate and
Premium Sales Department at 1-800-221-7945, extension 5442, or by email at
MacmillanSpecialMarkets@macmillan.com.

www.fsgbooks.com
www.twitter.com/fsgbooks • www.facebook.com/fsgbooks

1   3   5   7   9   10   8   6   4   2

for my parents,
Mark Davis and Yueh-hsiu Chien

I have now long been aware that the persons I see about me are not "cursory contraptions" but real people, and that I must therefore behave toward them as a reasonable man is used to behave toward his fellows.

—Daniel Paul Schreber, *Memoirs of My Nervous Illness*

THE SCAPEGOAT

1 When Kirstie interrupted me I was in the break room. I had just sat down at the round, perpetually stained plastic table in the corner and was listening with satisfaction to the coffee maker as it began its quiet gurgle. Reluctantly I made a small gesture of greeting.

She asked if it was a "fresh pot," and I nodded, and to discourage any further conversation I bent my head over the weekly paper that happened to be open on the table in front of me. She was dressed, I noticed, entirely in athletic clothing—black and elastic, with a muted sheen. Her cheeks were flushed, and the triangle of flesh below her collarbone was flecked with beads of perspiration.

She passed behind me and asked, startling me, "Is that the horoscopes?"

She moved closer to me and I could smell the scent of her freshly exercised body in the small, windowless room.

"That's funny," she said. She had not pegged me for the kind of man—the kind of "guy"—who read the horoscopes.

"Oh," I said quickly. "I'm not—I'm not reading this." And as I said it I saw that I looked like a very poor liar. I had failed to notice, somehow, that the paper in front of me had been turned to the horoscopes section, and not only that, but the facing page had been folded back with care.

"Could you read me mine?" she asked, reaching for a mug. "I'm a Pisces," she said, and my heart sank.

As a rule, I maintained a careful neutrality toward my colleagues. I preferred not to involve myself in university gossip, or department politics, aware, without regret, that I had chosen for myself a somewhat lonely stance. But when Kirstie arrived, early last year, I found that she provoked in me a strong aversion that I couldn't shake, an abiding hostility I could not explain even to myself. And yet, I thought, there was no real way to refuse her request, and so I found the right place on the page, next to a picture of two turning fish.

"'Wishful thinking won't make it so: don't waste any more time, energy, or resources on a dead end. You get your point across better by keeping your dignity. Some people just aren't buying what you're selling.'"

I thought of something else just then, and when I became aware of Kirstie again I saw that she was sitting back on her heels in front of the cabinet below the sink, as if momentarily frozen in place, her gaze apparently fixed on an unremarkable strip of wood below the sink's lip.

"Was that really," she asked, her voice suddenly very quiet, "what it said?"

I could not quite see how to answer her, and I was grateful when the coffeepot switched itself off with its distinct click and Kirstie seemed to forget her question and revive.

What I meant to do next was turn the page quickly, to forget all about horoscopes and Kirstie. This was not a day, after all, when I could afford to be distracted. But somehow, contrary to my intention, I saw my own index finger slide quickly down the page to rest on a crude drawing of a goat.

Dear Capricorn, the text read, *don't be afraid to connect the dots. The path between events that may seem unrelated will soon become clear. With your moon in the fifth house, you will find yourself uniquely positioned to set things in motion.*

When I had finished reading, I looked up at the wall. Somewhere, as if far away, Kirstie was stirring something into her cup and making some quiet remark, but I could barely hear it. I looked back down at the paper. I read my horoscope again. *The path between events that may seem unrelated will soon become clear . . .*

It was all very odd. The horoscopes had turned out to be something very different than I'd expected them to be. *Uniquely positioned*, I thought, *to set things in motion*. As much as I lacked confidence in the source, the message could not reasonably be dismissed. It was not irrelevant at all. Could it be a coincidence, I wondered, that I had received this strange message on this day, the day of my father's open house? A strange message, undoubtedly, and yet somehow encouraging.

My father—my late father, I should say—and I were not close at the time of his death, and our relationship had not been without its complications—and yet. And yet, I thought, as I rose from my seat and went out into the hallway, between a father and his only son, no matter the circumstances, runs a thread that should not be underestimated.

I put my hand out absently to my mailbox as I passed it in the hall; it was empty. My mind slipped, then, to the dream I'd had the night before the start of winter quarter, a peculiar dream in which I saw my father shoot himself on a bridge above a churning gray river. I also saw a hearse and cars creeping along Palm Drive, spooling out along the Oval, heading toward Memorial Church.

In the thin half-light of the next morning, I'd had a lingering sense of unease. It was just a dream, I told myself, although I'd seen that river before, I thought with a wry smile, I would recognize that bridge if it were coming down a dark alley with its collar turned up against the cold; it had featured in more of my previous dreams than I could count, though never, it was true, in conjunction with my father. What could it mean? I had not dreamt of my father since I was a child.

As I walked down the hallway toward the break room that morning I could not shake the feeling that even if the events in my dream did not conform precisely to real life, surely they did not mean nothing at all? Perhaps there had been some important change. It could, I thought— But there I stopped myself; dreams were dreams, and that was—

Consumed by my own train of thought, I had burst somewhat unceremoniously into the break room, where a group of graduate students, occupying all four chairs at the round plastic table, turned to me, startled, like children interrupted at a forbidden game. Now that I thought of it, I had the impression that they had been talking quite noisily just the moment before, and on my arrival had been struck dumb. One of them—Weber, I thought, was his name, a fey and bespectacled little Italian—turned to his neighbor and muttered, under his breath.

"Eccolo," he said. "Il fratellastro."

2 Needless to say, since my father's death he had been very much in my thoughts. There is always some regret, I would imagine, when there is a sense that where there might have been connection between family members there was strain, with death's finality precluding any rapprochement.

And it was not just thoughts of my father himself that were foremost in my mind; it was the circumstances surrounding his death that nagged at me. The more I considered them, the stranger they seemed. Not only that, but someone was trying to tell me something about these circumstances, or so I thought, because a copy of the local paper had appeared in my mailbox some weeks ago, its pages turned to the real estate section, the listing for my father's house circled in red pen. Who had done that, and why?

These were the thoughts that preoccupied me as I sat in my car across the street from my father's house—his former house, I should say, recently vacated. A woman was emerging from the front door holding a single balloon. She moved briskly down the path to tie it to the FOR SALE sign that sat like a grounded white bird on the lawn. The real estate agent, I thought, as she straightened up and, turning her back to me, looked up at the house.

And why hadn't he—my father—wanted to live on campus?

The house before me was a blue two-story affair of no particular style, with white trim and a shingled roof. It was at the end of a quiet cul-de-sac, deserted at this midday hour. I watched as the real estate agent adjusted her skirt, squared her shoulders, and went back up the pathway and closed the front door behind her. My father had been enjoying his third marriage when he died, and he had lived in this house with his young family.

I crossed the street, walked up the path, and rang the doorbell. Through the pane of frosted glass in the front door I could see the figure of the real estate agent advancing, and I felt a tingle of anticipation. This was all about to begin, I thought, as the door swung open and we were suddenly face-to-face. What had that horoscope said again? *You will find yourself uniquely positioned to set things in motion?* We shook hands, and she introduced herself as Sharon.

"If you wouldn't mind stepping onto this," she said, pointing to a white paper doormat that lay inside the threshold. It was printed in blue with the outlines of two footprints. "They just refinished the floors."

It was true, I thought, as I stepped carefully on, then off the paper mat, that the floors looked waxy and bright. There was cream-colored carpet on the stairs and a second-story landing, and that, too, looked freshly cleaned. In general, I thought, looking around me, the house had the appearance of having been polished within an inch of its life.

"Well," said Sharon. "Shall we start upstairs?"

Without waiting for an answer, she began to climb the

steps that curved up from the foyer to the second floor. She was older than I had expected; her youthful figure, as I'd seen it from the window of my car, had been deceptive. Up close, she was near my own age.

Another detail of note, I thought, as I followed her up the stairs, was that a strong scent of cinnamon had just been sprayed everywhere; with every other breath I caught another dose of it. This was disappointing; there was no connection between my father and a smell like that.

"Four bedrooms," Sharon was saying. "Three up, one down."

She cast a backward glance in my direction. "The previous owners used the downstairs bedroom as a study."

The previous owners, I thought. Now that I had started down this path there was no changing it—I would see it through to the bitter end.

Now she turned into what was obviously a child's room, a little girl's, with a single bed, a pink lamp on a white nightstand, and purple rocking horses on the wallpaper.

"Have you been looking long?" asked Sharon. She was standing by the door, watching me. I crossed the room to the closet and slid the door open. It was empty save for one additional lamp, the twin of the one on the nightstand, its cord wrapped around itself.

"Looking long?" I repeated.

"For a home."

Oh yes, I thought, of course. Looking for a home. In my excitement I had forgotten that this was, in fact, the customary reason to attend an open house.

"No," I said truthfully. "Not long."

"Well," said Sharon, when it became clear I did not intend to elaborate. "It's an excellent place to start."

I murmured my agreement and crossed the room again. Surely we had spent enough time at this point, in this irrelevant room, but she gave no signs of moving and instead I went to the window, which overlooked an unremarkable backyard: a lawn, a patio, a table with a green umbrella. Here my father had barbecued, presumably. Sharon, taking her cue, had moved across the room to position herself by my side, so that we stood shoulder to shoulder, and I noticed something strange about her arm. Her wrist, both wrists, in fact, were covered in thin silver bracelets, some inlaid with turquoise, but that was not the strange thing. From her left wrist to her left elbow stretched a long, thin scar, as if someone had drawn a needle along it. When she saw me looking at it she turned quickly away.

"That's half an acre down there," she said, and when she reached the door she turned. She had recovered herself. "Shall we move on?"

"Are you familiar with the area?" she asked, as we moved down the hallway. "I noticed your accent."

What a busybody Sharon was, I thought. What a little investigator.

"Oh yes," I said. "I've lived here for quite some time."

I mentioned the name of the university, and my employment there.

"Oh," she said, clearly impressed. "Then I should probably

call you Doctor. Do you by any chance know my brother-in-law?"

She named him, an orthopedist; I did not.

My capacity for this kind of chat was waning, and I opened a closet in the hallway. Inside it was ski equipment, a disco ball, and what appeared to be an Easter basket filled with miniature bottles of shampoo.

"Whose things are these?" I said, perhaps a little more sharply than I had intended.

"Yes, well," said Sharon. "The previous owners had to move unexpectedly, and some things were left behind. It will all go, though, eventually—"

"Is that so?" I said. "Why was that?"

"Why was what?"

"Why did they have to move," I asked, "so unexpectedly?"

"I'm not sure," said Sharon, but I noticed she was looking fixedly at a point above my shoulder and could not quite meet my gaze.

She knows, I thought.

"Just between you and me—" Sharon began, and then we were interrupted by a high-pitched shriek that I recognized after a moment as the more pedestrian sound of the doorbell. She frowned.

"Excuse me," she said. "Would you like to come down . . . ?" She gestured vaguely in the direction of the stairs.

"No, thank you," I said. "I'll stay up here."

She gave me a strange look, but said, "Of course," and hurried out of the room to the sound of the doorbell ringing again, and I heard her footsteps on the stairs in quick descent.

I moved slowly down the hallway, opening doors. Below me I could hear Sharon saying, "Hello," and then, "Well, *hel*-lo!" and I realized by her tone that she was addressing a child.

I stepped into a bathroom and shut the door. I stood still for a moment and tried to quiet my thoughts. The cabinets were empty, a disappointment; everything was white and silver and gleaming, and on the sink next to the faucet was a circle of soap in a little paper jacket. I could hear the trill of Sharon's voice and her footsteps coming up the stairs. Think, I told my reflection: you won't be able to stay at this open house forever—how to proceed?

As I came back out onto the landing, I caught a glimpse of the obedient little group of men and women who were following Sharon to the top of the stairs. There was no child, I thought distractedly, I must have misheard.

One of the newcomers was a man, older than myself, quite handsome and distinguished-looking in a dark V-neck sweater and with a full head of silver-gray hair. As he passed me on the landing, our eyes met—what eyes! I thought—and I felt a cold current of electricity pass between us.

What was that?

But the moment had passed, and I heard him say something to someone in front of him, not in English—French, I thought, or German.

I could not account for the look that had passed between us—it was not the kind of casual glance you gave to a stranger, but something else entirely. Whatever it had been, I thought, I did not have time to consider it now; I waited until the entire party had filed into the little girl's room, to look out, no doubt, at the unremarkable garden. Not a face I would forget, I thought, thinking of the silver-haired man. But I did, in fact, forget it, or any rate I did not remember it well the next time I saw it. But then I was at the end of the hallway, pushing open the door to what appeared to be the master bedroom. And for the first time since I'd arrived at the open house, I began to feel some hope that here a trace of my father still remained.

I closed the door quietly behind me. This room had a more lived-in quality, as if its occupants might still return, although it was difficult to imagine my father sleeping beneath the pastel print of a sailboat that hung above the bed. But there was a door off the far side of the room that turned out to be a closet still full of clothing. Coats, mostly, I was surprised to see.

Why, I wondered, so many coats in this climate? I ran a light hand across their sleeves. It occurred to me that in fact I *had* seen my father in a coat, once, but that had been many years ago, in practically another lifetime. The memory of the morning he'd come to visit me in Ottawa, where I had been living at the time, hovered just beyond my consciousness, threatening to intrude. But that was a complicated memory in many ways—and at this time, during this short window of opportunity in my father's house, it could only be a distraction. I made a somewhat dramatic gesture of frustration, as a consequence of which I found myself at the back of the closet, my face buried in the wool sleeves of my father's coats, my nose in contact with a stiff lapel, with only the vaguest sense of there being a noise behind me, a nagging, persistent noise, which eventually resolved itself into the voice of the real estate agent saying, "Sir? Sir?"

Here's a tip you won't need: It's always better to eat a little something, even when you think you aren't hungry. Especially when one lives alone, because it's easy to think to oneself: Why go through all that trouble, and dirty up dishes? But I have learned from experience that it's better to make an effort, even when the only beneficiary is yourself.

Which is why, when I returned home from my father's open house, I poured myself a glass of seltzer from the fridge and made myself something simple to eat. I put two slices of bread in the toaster and mixed a tin of salmon with mayonnaise, salt, and pepper. When the toast was done I spread a thick layer of salmon on each piece, arranged them on a plate, and took it to the dining room table, where I sat down in my customary seat facing the bay window, where I liked to watch the fog roll in from the sea.

I had just set my plate and glass down on the table when a small flash of red caught my eye. The light on the telephone was blinking, and upon closer examination I saw that the number in the little window was now an illuminated 2. I have two voice messages, I thought, with some surprise. I lifted my finger to press the button marked play—and hesitated. Would it be better, perhaps, to wait until after dinner? There was so much I needed to think over, and who knew—what I meant was, would it be more prudent to wait to introduce these new variables?

All the same, I thought, and pushed the button. The machine made its preliminary high-pitched beep, and then a youngish female voice filled the room.

"Hello," she said. "This is Jennifer calling from Dr. Fergu-son's office. Please let me know if there's a better number—" The machine squawked in protest as I brought my index finger down heavily on the button marked delete. *That*—an elab-orate piece of bureaucracy, due to a misunderstanding that arose the night I'd learned of my father's death—was certainly not something on which I would spend another moment. The telephone collected itself, beeped again, and Gerry Van Gelder's deep voice said:

"Hello there, it's Gerry."

He paused, clearing his throat, and I heard the faint rus-tling of papers in the background.

"Ann thought I should call and remind you about dinner on Friday—also to let you know that her father will be joining us; you met at Thanksgiving. We were thinking around . . ."

Not listening, I let the message play on to its finish. *No new messages*, pronounced the machine. The red number in the little window changed from 2 to 0.

I took my seat again at the table and spent the next min-ute or so not moving, staring out the window with no sense of what was on the other side of it. Gerry Van Gelder with an invitation to dinner, of course. It had been ridiculous to expect otherwise. Nothing to consider there; this was not a new vari-able at all, but a very old one.

I took a sip of seltzer and a bite of my sandwich, and let my mind wander. Most nights I put something on: the televi-sion, or the radio—always a talk station; human voices, even disembodied, can make a night a little easier to bear. But on that night, the night of my father's open house, I had no need for any distractions, and I ate in silence.

Little by little, it grew dark. Dusk turned the fading daylight gray-purple, then black. The fog crept up the lawn, toward the window, reaching its long white fingers through the pines, and as it did I felt my mind slowly empty.

The closer the white fog came, the more passive I grew, and when it was pressed thickly against the windowpane, moisture beading on the inside of the glass, I felt the tightly wound coil of the day's anticipation begin to unwind. Then I set my plate and glass to the side and took out the item I'd retrieved from the pocket of my father's coat at the open house—a piece of notepaper, folded in half, which I put on the table and smoothed open with my palm.

I saw at once that it was a piece of stationery from a hotel, the Old Mission Hotel San Buenaventura. The name appeared at the top of the square, and above it a crude drawing of a steeple, its two long fingers meeting in a point beneath a simple cross.

Written on it, in my father's near-illegible hand, were the words *Saturday, 10 am, MC.* Nothing more.

MC, I thought. MC. A person? A place? In either category, nothing came to mind. Tomorrow, I decided, I would think.

I turned the piece of paper over, but the other side was blank.

By then it had grown too dark to see, and I got up to switch on the light, and then sat back down with a feeling of satisfaction. I had been right to go to the open house, I was certain. I had the impression, somehow, that things were beginning to move. It was just as if— I checked myself. Did I want to think, again, of my horoscope? That unwelcome moment of intimacy I'd shared with Kirstie that morning in the break room?

There was something unsavory about it, and yet the temptation was strong. What was it that the horoscope had said? That the path between unrelated events would soon become clear. *Well.* The message was impossible to ignore. I was uniquely positioned, I thought, to set things in motion. Some headway was being made in the matter of my father's death.

When I had washed and dried the dishes, I made my way down the long hallway to the bedroom, undressed, and wandered into the bathroom to brush my teeth. With the light off, in the mirror, my naked torso was pale and luminous, soft in the middle and punctuated by two dark, disk-like nipples, a sparse V of hair between them. How repulsive I had grown in my middle age.

Did I already have a glass of water on the nightstand? I did. I turned on my reading light, got into bed, and reached for my book, a Swedish police novel I had recently begun. The chief detective was a divorced man with unhealthy eating habits and a weakness for Maria Callas. It seems that every detective novel I read now features this policeman, whose nationality varies, but who is dependably bitter and divorced, opera his soul's only worldly solace.

3 Despite my good intentions, over the next few days I made very little progress. I worried away at several far-fetched ideas about the initials MC, with no success.

And still I clung to the message in the horoscope. Perhaps it could still be true that I had set something in motion. And I was right. Still, it was not until several weeks after the open house that I made my next measurable advance.

I slept badly and woke before dawn that morning, then rose and ate a bowl of cereal in the dark. The panes of the bay window were covered in a thick blackness, with condensation clinging to their insides. I had hoped to catch the sunrise going over the reservoir—that can always give a welcome boost—but a thick fog had blanketed the valley, like a layer of cotton wool, and the day slid in gray and melancholy from the night, with little fanfare.

I made an uneventful pot of coffee in the break room, and as I was walking back to my office with my second mugful, I put my hand out reflexively to the inside of my mailbox, where my fingers brushed against a single sheet of paper. It had not been there when I'd left the day before.

It was a flyer printed on peach-colored paper, advertising a performance of Mahler's *Kindertotenlieder* at the hospital. The first in a series of lunchtime concerts, it said, and dimly I remembered that there had been a series like it before, several years ago, which I had never attended. And why not? I wondered, as I stood in the quiet hallway, steam rising from my coffee. I appreciated classical music, unlike the majority of my colleagues, and one could not have asked for a more convenient location. A concert, I thought, pleased by the idea, at lunchtime. A performance of the *Kindertotenlieder*. It seemed just the kind of thing I would enjoy. I looked at the flyer again and saw that the date of the concert was Friday, the very next day.

I made my way back to my office and sat down at my desk, lost in thought, when something moving outside the window caught my eye. A figure was bobbing along the path that ran next to the building—a jogger, I realized, a woman. And after a few aimless moments of watching her, I saw that the jogger was Kirstie.

The sky behind her was just beginning to lighten, and a faded orange light was showing through. She was wearing a dark windbreaker over her elastic pants, and fluorescent sneakers, her heels cutting cleanly through the air behind her as she made her way past the rows of empty parking spaces, out toward the center of campus. She did not appear to be moving very quickly, but her stride was regular and soothing to watch. The morning was crisp and cold, and I could see my breath on the windowpane in small white blooms.

How long I stayed like that I can't recall—a strange, slack feeling had spread throughout my limbs—but it must have been until I became aware that the telephone on my desk was ringing, and I started back from the window as if I had been caught in a compromising pose.

"Hello?" I said, regretting that I hadn't paused to let my breath grow more even.

It was a colleague of mine, calling to see if I was available for dinner. He was sorry for the late notice, he explained, but he was in charge of putting together a dinner party for a guest lecturer and was in need of one more person. Was I available?

Was I available? I thought. I hesitated a moment. Had this phone call really been intended for me? But, I thought, was it really necessary to always be so self-sabotaging? Was there any real reason I could not graciously accept an invitation to dinner?

Still, I hesitated. I could say, convincingly enough, that I would need to check, and I could open up my datebook and pretend that the snowy expanse inside was in fact filled with engagements. But, in the end, what would be the point of that? Yes, I said, I could make it; I would meet them at the restaurant at seven. I replaced the phone in its cradle and turned toward the window. Kirstie was gone, and the gray in the sky had burned off to reveal an equivocal blue.

And why, I asked myself, did I need to fret so about an invitation to dinner? I was cordial with many members of the department, more than I could count. And yet I could not help but feel a certain shameful pleasure. I felt—the thought is distasteful to me now—flattered by the invitation.

Which is not to say that I had illusions about it. It was clear to me even then that I had most likely been asked as a last-minute replacement for some other person, someone more naturally inclined to the company of others, and less remote from the department's social universe. But all the same, I thought, I had certain professional obligations. And perhaps it was . . . a renewal of something. Perhaps if I had not been the first choice of dinner guest, I also had not been the last.

The guest lecturer turned out to be a woman, of the heavily made-up, sand-colored variety. Her décolletage had been squeezed into a tight lavender suit jacket. She was, she explained, from Colorado.

"I imagined it would be so warm here," she said, shaking her head incredulously. "California! I thought. You know how you imagine it. I tried to go to the beach! I had to wear the sweater I brought for the plane!"

We (myself and my two colleagues, whom I knew only slightly) nodded appreciatively.

"And the fog!" she went on. "I could barely find the rental car this morning!"

We murmured our condolences politely, and I thought: It is one thing to be surprised, even pleased, by an unexpected invitation to dinner, and another thing entirely to attend. It's easy to forget, when one is so much alone, just how taxing the company of other people can be. And as the meal went on, the guest lecturer, no doubt delighted to find herself in a strange restaurant, in a strange city, in the company of three men, grew increasingly voluble and intoxicated. By dessert she was holding forth on a minor issue of internal politics at her home institution, pausing only to ferry spoonfuls of baklava into her open mouth and wipe its corners daintily with her napkin. There was a tangible feeling of relief when the check came, was perfunctorily fussed over and paid, and we all went out into the dark night, where the air was cold and sweet.

"Where did you say you were staying?" one of my colleagues asked our female companion, barely concealing a yawn.

"Oh, what *is* it called," said the guest lecturer with a laugh, as if to say: *Look at scatterbrained old me!* And then, with curious sharpness: "The Old Mission Hotel San Buenaventura."

"Oh right," he replied. "That's the one with the—you probably don't know, but there was a big thing about it, when they let *them* move in; in fact, some people say it was the nail in the coffin for our former—"

"No," interrupted my other colleague, in an unnecessarily loud voice, "I'm sure our guest is not aware."

The first man stared at him, flicked his eyes to me—and fell silent.

"No," he said sheepishly. "Right."

The guest lecturer rejoined with something I failed to hear, because the name of the hotel had arrested me, and for a moment I was unable to think clearly of anything. The folded piece of stationery I'd fished from my father's coat had had that name printed on it: the Old Mission Hotel San Buenaventura. The two fingers, meeting in a steeple, and above it the simple cross.

Somehow I'd fallen behind, and now I pushed forward to join the little trio; they were all standing at the edge of the parking lot, looking out toward the street. For all my haste to reach them I had not thought of what to say; would they still be on the subject of the hotel? I wondered, but as I approached I heard the guest lecturer ask:

"Is there anywhere you'd recommend going tomorrow morning? My flight isn't until five."

"Hmm," said one of them, moving aside so I could join them. "Well—"

"I've heard," she went on, and her eyes swung from him to me, her breathing audible in the silence of the parking lot, "that the redwoods are a must."

"Oh yes," I heard myself reply. Suddenly the parking lot had grown very still and dark; even the cars on the street in front of us seemed to be moving without sound.

"There's even one you can drive through? Is that true?"

She gave me a close look. It was clear that her question was meant particularly for me, and I was vaguely aware of the figures of my colleagues silently receding.

I struggled to speak for a moment. Of all the places she could have mentioned, why that one?

"Yes," I said slowly. "That's true, there is one you can drive through."

"Have you been there?"

"Yes," I admitted. "Once."

"Well, by the look on your face," said the guest lecturer teasingly, "it can't have been very fun."

"No," I said. "Well—it's been so long now, and I went there with a . . . with a friend, who was visiting me from Ottawa."

Astonishing, really, how painful that was still, I thought, like the pulse of an old toothache that is inexplicably revived.

It was unlike me to speak of such things. It was because of the hotel; it had thrown me off course.

"Ottawa," she said, eyebrows raised. "Is that in Canada?" I could see that my stumble over "friend" had not escaped her, as incapacitated as she was. "Is *that* where your accent is from? You're Canadian?"

"No," I said. "British, but that was very long ago."

"I see," she said. "Your accent's very faint."

The conversation, if it could be called that, was threatening to peter out.

"Hadn't we better find your car?" I said.

"Yes, probably," she replied, and smiled mysteriously. Then she took a few uncertain steps away from me, looking with expectation over the sea of parked cars.

"It's a white car," she said, apparently to herself.

"Are you sure you're feeling up to driving?" I asked, having merely voiced the question that would have been on anyone's mind, watching her shift her weight unsteadily from spine-heeled shoe to shoe.

The guest lecturer stopped, paused, and turned around. A smile spread slowly across her wide mouth, to which new lipstick had been recently and inexpertly reapplied.

"No," she said. "You're right. Anyone can see I'm not up to it at all. Would you mind taking me to my hotel?"

We drove west, cutting through campus.

"Are those . . ." slurred my passenger, "those palm trees? The famous ones?"

It was a dark night, and a crescent moon was visible above the roof of Memorial Church. We turned right into the Arboretum, and I sensed the guest lecturer sitting up a little straighter in her seat.

"Is that," she said, more distinctly, "where the dead son is buried?"

I looked over at her, startled, and then I saw that she was squinting through the dark at the white form of the mausoleum.

"Yes," I said. "I think so, yes."

"So sad," said the guest lecturer in a mournful voice. "They told us all about it on the tour. *The children of California shall be our children.*"

She gave me a sideways look, as if this quotation from our university's founder might have particularly impressed me.

"That's right," I said, and then we were spat out on the other side of campus at the base of the foothills heading north past the golf course.

"He died of typhus?"

"Ty*phoid*, I think," I replied.

What a strange thing she wanted to talk about, I thought. I had not anticipated discussing the century-old death of a boy from typhoid as if it were recent news, and to call it "so sad" did not seem quite appropriate, but it was often the case, I remembered, that tourists were most interested in this somewhat morbid aspect of our institution's founding.

"I think I know where we are now," said the guest lecturer, pulling herself upright with effort. The headlights swept along a vast expanse of yellowed grass. In the darkness it glowed pale and eerie against the black sky, as if we were crisscrossing the foothills of some other planet.

"Even this," said the guest lecturer, indicating the land around us, "belongs to the university?"

I nodded.

"And can't be sold."

I looked at her again. I doubted that I had ever met anyone who'd shown such interest in the campus tour.

"Right again," I said. "Only leased."

"Here it is," she said abruptly, and I turned into an unmarked driveway, flanked on either side by a thick hedge of oleander. The plants were so tall, and the path so gently winding, that it was only when we had come around the very last bend that the hotel itself rippled into view: low, white, and crouching like a cat. It was lit dramatically from below, and I could see that it was that most ubiquitous of all Californian buildings, a stucco building with a red tile roof.

From its center rose the modest steeple, and above it, the simple cross. I felt a throb in my wrists, and my pulse skipped forward. A strange new quality established itself in my mind. Two fingers, I thought, and I saw the image of the drawing on the notepaper superimposed on the steeple in front of me, as if that one, the drawing, was the one that counted.

We pulled up to the front entrance. Out of the corner of my eye I noticed a remarkably tall bellhop standing behind a podium, eyeing us with no visible reaction as we slowed to a stop.

Here I was, I thought; now, how do I get inside?

There was no reason I could not simply come back another day, I reasoned, it was not as though my father's body were upstairs growing cold—no—whatever there was to be gleaned from this hotel, if there was anything, could be learned just as successfully tomorrow or the next day. Now that I knew where it was, I could—

I was startled from my thoughts by a sudden soft pressure on my knee. Looking down, I saw that it was the hand of the guest lecturer.

Through the windshield I could see the bellhop, who was coming slowly toward the guest lecturer's door. Evidently, he had decided we were in need of assistance. He put his hand on the door handle and pulled it open, and I was surprised by the look he gave us through the glass—there was nothing friendly about it, and perhaps even something faintly menacing. Then he stepped back, holding the guest lecturer's door open, and his face was plunged into shadow again.

The guest lecturer, however, was oblivious to all this. She gave the bellhop a look of unmistakable displeasure and, without saying a word, reached out and shut her door again.

"Now," she said, replacing her palm on my knee. "Would you like to come up and have a drink?"

She was breathing, as she said the words, rather heavily, and on each exhalation rode the sweet-sour smell of wine.

I found I could not reply immediately. Instead, I looked

down at her hand. I could feel the warm, sticky heat of her palm through the fabric of my pants, and I felt a nearly incapacitating desire to push it off. But, I thought, now is not the time to be so particular.

The guest lecturer, I could feel, was looking at me expectantly, waiting for an answer. Look, I asked myself sternly, is this an investigation of a death? Or not?

I watched with a feeling of detachment as my own hand released itself from the steering wheel and came to rest on top of the guest lecturer's, covering it like a shell on a snail. To have done so felt nothing short of heroic, as though with this one gesture I had swept all the stars and the moon from the sky. Then I brought my gaze to meet hers, and lifted the corners of my mouth in a smile.

"I would like that very much," I said.

"Isn't this lobby bizarre?" whispered the guest lecturer, as we stepped across the threshold.

It was, and in a way I had not expected. To begin with, its entire visible staff (besides the bellhop outside) seemed to consist of one dark-haired young man, a small and fastidious-looking person, who nodded politely to the guest lecturer as she tottered by, aiming a little wave of her fingertips in his direction.

But stranger by far was the look of the lobby, which was incongruously ultra-modern, as if someone who had never seen the outside of the building had ordered up an interior design scheme from some other hotel, one located in some sleek metropolis. Everything was hushed and dimly lit. On our right, white leather donut-shaped couches curved around low black tables, and on our left was a long, narrow bar that had been lined with a row of tiny red votive candles.

There were about half a dozen seats at the bar, all of them empty, nor was there any sign of a bartender, though liquor bottles were lined up against the mirrored wall, and clean glasses gleamed brightly from their shelves. Nothing about the place—I looked around me once more, noting the scent-lessness of the air, the soft, piped-in music—had any speci-ficity. The guest lecturer and I could have been making our way across a lobby in London or Dubai; there was no way of knowing in what larger geographical region we would find ourselves if we stepped outside.

"A lot of controversy," the guest lecturer was saying, "about it opening. Did you hear about that?"

I shook my head. I had not heard about any controversy; I had not heard anything about this hotel at all. I was not even aware that it had opened, but that did not trouble me in the slightest. Even if I had been, I would not have been interested in discussing it with the guest lecturer. No! All I wanted, in that particular moment, was a little quiet in which a new thought could take form. My own father had walked here—exactly here, where I was walking!—from the front door of the Old Mission Hotel through the lobby to the elevator.

How often could one say that one had walked—*actually walked*—in someone else's footsteps? If this did not bring me closer to some understanding of my father's death, what would?

We had reached the elevator, the doors slid open, and we entered. I was surprised to see that the numbers on the but-tons went all the way up to 5.

"Five floors?" I said aloud. "It's much taller than it looks from the outside."

Whether the guest lecturer heard me or not, I couldn't have said—she was engaged in a careful inspection of her own face in the mirrored back wall of the elevator. At one point she pulled back her lips in what I at first thought was an especially menacing smile, until I realized that she was trying to see if there was anything stuck in her teeth. I cleared my throat loudly to remind her of my presence, but she paid me no attention whatsoever until we had entered her hotel room, Room 409, where, after rummaging in her handbag for the key, and then opening the door, she made a beeline for the bed, seated herself heavily on the edge, and kicked off her shoes with an air of satisfaction. Beneath her considerable bosom the lavender suit jacket strained at the buttons.

The room, like the lobby, was utterly devoid of any distinguishing characteristics. Everything you'd expect in the way of hotel furnishing was there, and nothing more: a bed, a desk, a cabinet with a television, and a wall of windows obscured by a heavy ocher curtain.

The guest lecturer cocked her head to one side and regarded me with feigned criticism. "What are you doing all the way over there?" she said. "You're so far away."

I could, I wanted to say, hardly be described as far away. I was standing in front of the television and could have grazed her knee with one fingertip if I'd reached out, but instead I made an attempt at laughter and said that I had been promised a drink, and made a show of looking around me as if one might appear.

The guest lecturer raised her hands up in a gesture of

defeat, and then brought them down rapidly so that they slapped against her thighs. She liked this so much, apparently, that she did it again: flinging her arms up and then slapping them down again with gusto.

"There's gin in the cabinet," she said thickly, gesturing toward the wall, a wall where, as far as I could see, there was nothing in the way of furniture.

"I think you have a message," I said, because I had come across the room to the desk, where a many-buttoned telephone sat, the red light blinking next to an image of an envelope.

"Humph," said the guest lecturer indistinctly. "Probably my kids."

She was beginning to lean backward, little by little, like an ocean liner sinking below the wave line, until she was lying prone on the bed.

"Do you have kids?" she asked suddenly.

"I don't," I said.

"Ever been married?"

"No."

The guest lecturer muttered something into the bedspread, something that sounded like, "Lucky."

"I have five," she said, her voice suddenly distinct. "Kids."

She was lying on her back, looking up at the ceiling, her feet in their pantyhose splayed in front of her at the end of the bed.

"My husband and I are both only children, and we thought growing up was a little lonely, you know? Let's have a big family. Everyone will be friends."

I nodded, though I knew she couldn't see me. The idea sounded reasonable enough.

She laughed darkly. "They all hate each other."

I began to imagine the guest lecturer's five children, sandy-haired like their mother, standing on the lawn outside their home in Colorado—and then I found I had no interest in imagining them at all.

"How about you?" she said, turning on the bedspread to face me, a maneuver which caused one of her breasts to pour out over the other, as if suffocating it.

"How about me what?"

"Do you have siblings?"

I shook my head. "No."

"Oh yeah?" she said. "So you had a lonely childhood, too."

I shrugged. I had never quite succumbed to the habit, so dear to the American heart, of casually trading confidences.

"What are your parents like?" she said doggedly. The question put a stop, temporarily, to my whirring thoughts, and I was unhappily transported to the last visit I had paid my mother, her room suffocatingly hot, and the nurse, cool and efficient, bringing me a piece of gauze and a wet washcloth for my nosebleed. *It's the desert air*, the nurse had said. *Pinch it here at the bone.*

"That's a funny question," I said.

The guest lecturer raised her eyebrows in surprise. "I think it's pretty standard."

When I spoke again I felt my voice was coming through a little strangely, like a familiar song played just half an octave off.

"They were never married," I said. "I grew up with my mother."

"Oh," said the guest lecturer. "In England?"

"In England," I repeated.

This woman, I thought, feeling irritated, is nothing but a big distraction. I looked down at her supine form with distaste.

"Any more questions?"

I had spoken perhaps more harshly than I had intended. I came to the side of the bed and knelt down, so that she and I were at eye level. Her eyes widened and grew more alert.

"You look tired," I said. "Why don't you go to sleep?"

Her eyebrows raised questioningly. She was breathing audibly through her nose but did not speak.

"That's right," I said. "Go to sleep."

Her eyes closed. The furrows in her brow smoothed themselves over, and her features seemed to settle slightly and grow less tense. Several minutes later, I heard the beginnings of a gentle snore.

Well, I thought, this is lucky, as I watched the lapels of the lavender suit jacket rise and fall. The whole evening had been unbelievably lucky, in fact. One thing had led so easily to the next, and now the most unpleasant part of it had just fallen asleep, fully clothed, on her bed. I could not have asked for a kinder set of circumstances. I was now free, I reflected, to move about the room, to examine it for clues.

Clues! I smiled a small, private smile to myself. What a childish word to use. But all the same.

On the other hand, I thought, as I rose to my feet and began to move slowly about the small, generic room, perhaps it's unwise to overstate it; this was *not* a crime scene, I reminded myself. My father, that he had been to this hotel, that was likely to be true. And kept a souvenir, also true. And here was a good question: Why? There was something inherently suspicious about a man in need of a hotel room in the same city in which he lives. That was undeniable.

But I had no way of knowing which room he had stayed in. If it had been this one, the coincidence would be remarkable—and even so, it would have since been cleaned and inhabited; a thousand different people could have stayed in it.

I moved to the heavy ocher curtain and drew it back slightly, revealing only a view of the parking lot under the black night sky, flanked by the long oleander hedge. I began to feel somewhat discouraged, and my investigation of the room did not improve my mood. Peering into the darkness at the dim forms, I came to no judgment more noteworthy than my initial one: that it was a small and suitably furnished hotel room, outfitted in the same new and impersonal style as the lobby, though less aggressively modern.

The desk! I thought. At least there is the desk! There could be something there. I walked over to it and, taking care to do so quietly, pulled open the drawer. Inside was a bundle of writing paper and envelopes. Each sheet was the twin of the one I had at home—a square of notepaper with the simply drawn cross and steeple. I traced one slowly with my finger.

I imagined my father, standing where I stood, sliding open the drawer of the desk, taking out a sheet of writing paper, writing on it—here was a complimentary pen: *Saturday, 10 am, MC*. Perhaps he had been on the phone? With MC himself? Herself?—then folding it in half and putting it in the pocket of his coat.

Is that what happened? I asked myself. And why? Why, I thought, was he wearing a coat in the first place?

I slid the drawer shut, then opened it again, removed a sheet of notepaper from the bundle, folded it in half, and put it in the pocket of my pants. There, I thought. Now what has that achieved? I felt like a member of a cargo cult, who, after donning his wooden headset, gazes up from a straw control tower at an empty sky, without the faintest idea of what to expect.

There must be something I was missing. It occurred to me then that the sound of snoring had stopped, and I looked over at the guest lecturer, half certain she'd be propped up on one elbow, watching me at my probably pointless ritual. But she was not; she was as laid out on her back as ever, only now the rise and fall of the lavender suit jacket was imperceptible. But she might wake at any point. Perhaps, I thought, it was time for me to go. And it was then, as I slid the desk drawer shut and turned toward the door, that I stubbed my toe, and noticed the dark, solid object I had stubbed it on, which on closer examination was revealed to be a slim briefcase made of smooth brown leather that had been concealed in the shadowy recess below the desk.

Strange, I thought. Why would the guest lecturer feel the need to hide a briefcase beneath her desk?

I knelt and ran my fingers along its top, feeling the metal buckles. I looked over at the guest lecturer lying on the bed, at her earrings, at her brassy hair and wide mouth. I thought, The woman before me would not carry such a briefcase. The two simply did not go together. I ran my fingertips along the buckles again. There was no lock. All I had to do was desire it and the briefcase would open. I lifted it, ever so slightly, off the floor, and gave it a gentle shake—something inside made a heavy *clunk*. Whatever it was, it was certainly not made of paper.

But, I told myself, this was not, strictly speaking, a part of looking into my father's death. No reasonable argument could be made about its relevance. So what if a woman from Colorado, an unassuming woman, a somewhat coarse and unappealing woman, had found herself in possession of a lovely and apparently expensive briefcase? What did that have to do with me?

Nothing! I answered my own question sharply. The answer was nothing. And as I thought this, I saw that I had opened the briefcase.

At first I could not make out what was inside. The light was too dim under the desk, and I made an inelegant scooting movement backward toward the center of the room, so that the thick stripe of moonlight made by the gap between the wall and the heavy curtain lay across my lap. Now I could see the rough outlines of the object that lay at the bottom of the briefcase, but it was still not quite bright enough to distinguish it by sight. Cautiously, I touched the lining of the briefcase; I brushed lightly against it with my fingertips. It was made of a soft and delicate material—suede, I thought—that had been marred in places by a sticky substance. Even in the half-light I could see that these wet patches were darker than the rest.

I brushed lower down, and my fingers closed around a hard, curved object, extremely heavy for its size and a little longer than my hand, and held it up to the stripe of moonlight to see if I could get a better look. That was when the darkness in the room took on a new quality—it thickened, somehow, and grew more opaque; it pressed inward against me. I froze, the hard, sticky object illumined by the light. I could not escape the feeling that it was the point upon which all the attention of the darkness was focused.

You're imagining things, I told myself. Darkness doesn't have an attention. What is this you're holding? I asked myself. Concentrate! The thing I was holding appeared to be made of stone, a stone carving of an animal. Here was a tail, some crudely carved teeth, here the suggestion of low-set eyes. But what kind of animal it was meant to be was impossible to tell, because it was covered in a dark and viscous sludge, the same substance that had stained the lining of the briefcase. Wrapped around the carving was a thin piece of matter. I ran my fingers along it several times. I could not even say how long I remained with that object in my hand, anxiously tracing and retracing that long and peculiar filament with my fingertips, until the conclusion I'd been resisting struggled free and laid itself unequivocally across my thoughts. It was true, I thought—it felt very much like a human hair.

5 Concentrate! I told myself again, as I rode the elevator down to the lobby. Act natural! I stared at the buttons on the elevator control panel, I seared into them with the power of my gaze, as first the 3, then the 2, and then the L were illuminated, each like the pale orange glow of a cigarette tip glimpsed through the night.

That was no ordinary object! I thought. I put a hand out to the elevator wall, to steady myself.

And no ordinary hotel room! Now the button marked L was glowing, now it winked out.

My hands! I thought, for one panicked moment, before the doors opened, but when I brought them up to the light I was astonished to find that they were completely clean. There was nothing on them—not a spot. How could that be? But before I had a chance to take that thought any further, the elevator doors opened to reveal the lobby and a tired-looking young couple with a pair of wheeled suitcases. I stepped out to let them pass.

I was surprised to find that the lobby was deserted—just as it had been before—except for the dark-haired young man at the reception desk by the front door.

Why wasn't anyone there? I would have thought that this would be the hour for the bar and lounge to be, if not filled to the brim, at least frequented by a few patrons. But not only were there no patrons at all, but the bar gave every sign of having been closed up for the night—the stools had disappeared, and the votive candles that had been burning when I arrived were now extinguished and stacked behind the bar. How odd, I thought. I could not have spent more than—I thought—forty minutes upstairs, at the most, and in that time the bartender had apparently come and gone, and closed up shop?

"Good evening, sir."

The young man who'd been standing behind the reception desk materialized at my elbow.

In spite of all that I had recently experienced, I had a moment of amused surprise; it was not often that one was addressed with such formality in California.

"Can I help you with something?"

"No," I said. "Well, I was just wondering why there isn't anyone here at the bar."

"It's closed for the night," said the young man. "Sorry to disappoint you. Were you expecting someone?"

"No," I said. I looked over at the bar again, as if it might be able to assist, at the snuffed-out candles, arranged in orderly stacks. "I'm not expecting anyone.

"But it's only"—and I looked at my watch, as the young man regarded me placidly—"a quarter past nine," I said. "That seems a little early."

The young man's eyebrows rose, ever so slightly, like a pair of clouds moving in the sky. He pulled back his sleeve to look at his own watch. By the expression on his face, what he read there was just as he'd expected.

"Is it possible that your watch has stopped, sir?" He came

close to me now, wrist-first, and I could smell the hint of his cologne, something vaguely familiar.

"But," I said. I felt the situation was passing out of my control. I had a brief and shuddering reprise of the feeling I'd had upstairs in the guest lecturer's hotel room, of the darkness thickening around me, pressing in—but that, I thought, could not really have happened. I pushed the thought away from me firmly.

"Are you sure that's the time?" I said.

"Yes," said the young man smoothly. "I'm sure. The bar closes at eleven."

"At eleven," I repeated.

"That's right," he said.

We stood there in silence for a moment. "Is something wrong?" he asked.

I shook my head.

"It's only that I must have . . . lost track of time, somehow."

"Well," said the young man, smiling, "that, and your watch stopped."

His features, now that I was seeing them up close, were remarkably smooth and perfect—he was too delicate to be called handsome, but everything looked as though it had been made very carefully, with great attention to detail. What an unusual creature, I thought, remembering his "Good evening, sir"—he was certainly not from around here.

"I hope you had a pleasant stay," he said. Evidently, he had mistaken me for a hotel guest. "Do you need help with your car?"

"No," I said. What kind of help would I need? "Thank you, I'll be fine."

He stood, watching me, as I walked out of the hotel, and a million different questions suggested themselves. What was that thing in the briefcase, for one? And what could account for that . . . change in the atmosphere, upstairs? What had happened to the time, or rather, to my watch?

I glanced back over my shoulder at the hotel and saw that the impressively large bellhop had gone to stand by the little front desk man in the entryway. Backlit by the soft glow of the lobby lights, their silhouettes were comically mismatched— the bellhop huge and stoop-shouldered, the dark-haired young man tiny and still. I had the unsettling feeling that they—and perhaps the hotel itself—were watching me go.

It was a relief to be out in the night air, under the quiet sky, and the sudden drop in temperature gave my senses a welcome little shock. It was a relief, too, to have escaped the company of the guest lecturer; the moment in the car when she'd laid her hand on my knee had been particularly difficult. But, I thought, tomorrow she would fly back to Colorado, and I would never encounter her again. The piece of stationery! I thought. But when I felt anxiously in my pocket, I found it was still there.

I was so involved in these disjointed thoughts, flitting in and out of my consciousness like the chirruping of birds, that it was not until I came out from behind a dense bank of ole-ander that I saw, to my surprise, that tucked behind the wind-shield wiper of every car in the parking lot was a small orange piece of paper.

I stopped short. It is some kind of advertisement, or no-tice about parking, I told myself, but when I advanced warily upon my own vehicle, I saw that it was neither of those things, but something else, the half sheet filled with cramped, over-xeroxed handwriting. It was too dark outside to read it properly. I freed it, opened the car door, and flicked on the overhead light. I still had some idea that it was a communication from the hotel, but a moment's reading disabused me of that. At the top of the page, in block letters, appeared what seemed to be the "title" of the piece—*STOP SITES OF GENOCIDE FROM BECOMING TOURIST ATTRACTIONS SHAME on our university for this dirty deal! The wind of freedom blows but for whom, Mr President—* I stopped reading there, although it went on, the script growing more crowded and illegible with each line.

On the other side was a map of California in grainy black outline. All along the coast, angry red Xes had been marked. This is an odd piece of paper, I thought, it was not meant for me. I looked toward the entrance of the hotel, and I could see, to my surprise, through the gap in the oleander, that the bellhop and the dark-haired young man were still standing there, framed by the doorway.

From this distance, I told myself, there was a limit to what they could actually see, there must be. The parking lot, I saw with a quick glance, was deserted. With one hand I rolled down the window, and with the other I crumpled the little orange sheet of paper into a ball, then dropped it discreetly to the ground outside. Whatever that was, I thought, some crackpot's personal crusade, it did not concern me. There was a limit to how many bizarre events a person could take an interest in over the span of one evening.

6 I woke the next morning in my own bed, with the feeling that the explainable world was somehow slipping from my grasp. Bleak, gray morning light filled the room, and faintly I could hear the sound of birds. How—I thought—how could that all have happened? I turned over on my side to face the wall. What a remarkable series of events; I could barely believe in them.

I roused myself, got out of bed, put on my robe, and went into the kitchen to make a plate of toast. I was down to the heel of the loaf and its sad, curving neighbor; it took several attempts to make them look at all appealing. I sat down to eat at the table facing the bay window. As I chewed, I noticed that a glossy black bird with a yellow beak had landed on the lawn and was bobbing along through the grass, its beady eye trained on the ground below. It reminded me of something, though I could not remember what.

So many days and nights had passed without event, really, and then, all of a sudden, so much in one night. Though it was true that I had slept in the comfort of my own bed and been out of the house for only five or six hours, all told, I felt exhausted, like someone recently returned from an extended trip overseas.

From down the hallway I heard the muffled trill of my

alarm clock—I had forgotten to turn it off. I went back into the bedroom to flip the switch, and then, seeing the pants I'd worn the night before draped over my chair, I reached into the right-hand pocket and extracted the folded sheet of letter paper I'd retrieved from the guest lecturer's hotel room desk. Here was the proof, I thought, that I hadn't dreamed the whole thing!

I took it back with me to the kitchen, where I opened the drawer underneath the telephone and took out the piece of hotel notepaper I'd taken from my father's coat at the open house. With my palm I smoothed them both flat. As I'd suspected, except for the appointment—*Saturday, 10 am, MC*—they were identical. Two steeples, two simple crosses. With my index finger, I traced first one, and then the other.

Through the window, I could see the black bird was scratching madly in the dirt, a ball of frenzied determination, though whatever it was he had in his sights seemed perpetually out of reach. Inside my slippers my feet were clammy, and the two pieces of hotel stationery beside the telephone stared blankly at me, mockingly. Well, they seemed to say, so what? What exactly did your little escapade uncover? That your father stayed the night in a hotel? That the hotel still uses the same kind of stationery? That the hotel's traditional exterior belies an incongruous, Euro-modern lobby? What are you going to do—make a complaint about interior design?

Without warning, my thoughts skipped to the briefcase under the desk, the buttery feel of its leather, its macabre contents. What about *that*? The sticky residue? The strange quality of the darkness?

But, I thought, no! and shook the thought from me as a dog shakes water from its coat. That briefcase was of no relevance to me and my projects, there was no way in which it could be traced back to my father's death. I should not have opened it, I told myself sternly. That was all.

On my way to the break room later that morning, I saw that there was an envelope in my mailbox. I tore it open and read the contents as I put the coffee on to brew. It was a bill from the hospital. There had been a misunderstanding earlier this year, and a kind but clearly confused woman had mistaken a perfectly normal remark I had made for something more sinister. It was difficult to recall all the details, as that had been the night I learned of my father's death, when there were more important things on my mind. One cannot be held accountable for every little thing one says. It had not been my intention, as she had evidently thought, to do anything dramatic. Natural, wasn't it, I thought, as I puttered around the break room, to have been upset that night, and unfortunate that the old woman had misunderstood.

When, some time later, I returned to my office and looked at the clock, I registered that it was noon with little interest at first. Then I thought, Noon! And sprang up and pulled on my coat, sending the blinds scuttering down the window. Noon was the hour of the lunchtime concert of the *Kindertotenlieder*, and now even if I hurried I'd be late.

I pushed open the double doors of the breezeway and stepped out into the bright midday sunlight. Below me and to the right was the med school quad, with its green patch of lawn and trio of willows. Little groups of students were scattered here and there on the grass, eating their lunches. At least, I thought, as I stepped through the automatic doors that led to the hospital, I would be unlikely to encounter any of my colleagues at the concert; as a rule they would consider themselves too young and interesting for classical music.

The moving walkway deposited me on the second floor of the hospital, where I took the escalator down to the ground floor and was at once caught up in the densely moving mass of the building's main artery at the lunch hour. People holding bouquets of flowers tugged at the hands of small children, candy stripers manned their station, and doctors in scrubs, unencumbered, moved with greater purpose than the rest. Here and there one could even spot the sick themselves, dragging their oxygen tanks behind them in their slow and destinationless migration.

When I finally came to the rotunda I was disappointed to see that the performance was already underway. A pale, heavyset young man wearing a black satin cummerbund was standing on the raised semicircle reserved for performers and singing, his large white hands clasped in front of him. Behind him was an enormous arrangement of red gladiolas in a vase, and behind that was a two-story wall of windows that looked out onto the hospital's front driveway with its big, glittering fountain. There were no seats, I thought at first, with dismay, but after a moment I saw an unoccupied chair in the middle of a row and inched toward it, navigating my way carefully over pairs of feet and mouthing my apologies. Eventually, I found my way to the empty seat, sat down, and gratefully closed my eyes.

At first, I could hear nothing but the sound of my own pulse, throbbing in my temples. The flurry of activity had aroused me, and I found that my thoughts would not stop agitating themselves, like a dog tightly circling its own bed, never settling. This was particularly galling to me because it had been my intention to immerse myself fully in the music.

The music itself—that was another thing. The sound of the young man's voice singing something slow and sad came to me as if from very far away—as if I were standing in the depth of a valley, and the singer on the peak of a mountain.

There was another, more immediate noise, much closer, nonmusical. Someone was rustling a newspaper, of all things! Well, what can you expect? I thought. I had seen the audience before I'd shut my eyes: the vacant-eyed sick, the elderly, here and there an aloof, dark-skinned aide.

I redoubled my efforts to concentrate on the music . . . and was startled, genuinely startled, by the unmistakable sound of applause. My eyes flew open. The young man in the cummerbund was inclining his head in a very slight bow. His singing, I realized, had made almost no impression on me at all. Feebly, and feeling foolish, I joined in the tail end of the applause as the young man took his seat, and a sharp-featured young woman rose to take his place.

She positioned herself on the semicircle, adjusting the russet shawl she had wrapped around her shoulders, and gave a small, decisive nod to the piano player, a balding little man in a camel-colored sports coat whom I had not noticed until now. This new singer was slim, with blond hair and an Eastern European look about her. It occurred to me that one did not often see an opera singer of such slim stature. Was the sound better, I wondered, when it emanated from a more spacious architecture? Of course, it was not likely that the field's best and brightest would be performing at a hospital during the lunch hour. And—another question occurred to me—this *Kindertotenlieder*, could it properly be called an opera?

But here I was again in danger of being distracted by irrelevant questions, and this time I was determined to listen carefully to the music, and with that in mind I closed my eyes again for the full effect.

Could he not, I thought, several minutes later, and by *he* I meant not the piano player but Mahler, could he not have made this *Kindertotenlieder* just a little faster, a little livelier? Then the song might have caught my interest, but unfortunately it was neither of those things, rather it was slow, melancholy, and artless, just a lonely voice wandering up and down the scale, rising and falling with no particular design.

I had a little daydreaming scene just then, in which I stood in the parking lot of the restaurant, as I had the night before, with the guest lecturer, looking out with her over rows and rows of parked cars. It was very quiet in the daydream, as quiet as a tomb, and as chilly and dark, so that I could see the guest lecturer's breath clearly, in white puffs, as she said, with determination, "It's a white car."

Another noise nearby threatened to distract me—a sniffling, prefatory sound, like someone readying to blow their nose—but only for a moment. I tightened my grip on the daydream, in which, now, the guest lecturer and I were crossing the lobby of the Old Mission Hotel, that peculiar, scentless lobby. On our left was the empty bar, with its row of tiny red candles. *Did you hear,* the guest lecturer was saying, *about all the controversy with this place?*

Close by, the wet, sniffling noises were becoming more pronounced. The elderly! I thought. My god! Undoubtedly the worst kind of people.

All the controversy, I thought, returning to the daydream. *This dirty deal,* she had said. But now I was conflating two unrelated moments, I knew: what the guest lecturer had said as we stepped across the lobby, and what had been written on that piece of orange paper that I had found tucked behind my windshield wiper.

These things had the ring of some kind of importance, and yet if I was honest, at my core I felt no interest in them. It was disappointing that they interrupted me now. But before I could encourage my thoughts in an alternative direction, the song ended, there was a little peal of applause, and the concert was over.

Was that possible? I thought, astonished. Surely I had only been sitting here for . . . but then I realized that I had no sense of what amount of time had passed at all.

"How'd you like it?" said a female voice next to me. Even with my eyes closed I could tell it was the same person who'd sniffled loudly through the concert. Of course she would be just the sort of person who would also want to chat afterward, as we were all trapped in our seats. I opened my eyes briefly to look away from the voice and down the aisle, to see if there was any chance of escape, but at the other end of my row a gaunt and ancient man was refusing to be cajoled into a wheel-chair, and it was clear there would be no egress for some time.

Begrudgingly, I turned to my neighbor—and stopped short. She was not, as I had imagined, an old woman. Neither was she a stranger. She was Kirstie.

"Oh," I said, startled. "I'm sorry, I didn't realize it was you."

Her face, so familiar, was nearer to mine than it ever had been before, all the features I'd seen only in passing were now uncomfortably close: the slightly shiny, slightly wet lower lip, and disappearing upper one, the nose, and the wide-set, mildly bulbous eyes, which now registered a look of surprise.

"You didn't realize it was me?" she asked.

"No," I said.

In the intervening silence I noticed that she was dressed not in her athletic wear but, uncharacteristically, in actual clothing: a gray, form-fitting skirt and a cream-colored blouse with a soft ruffle curving down the middle. The effect, on her sturdy frame, was jarring.

"But," she went on, "I waved to you. I waved to show you that the seat next to mine was empty."

"I can assure you," I said icily, "if you did wave, I didn't see it. I saw myself that this seat was empty."

Kirstie stared at me. After a moment, she laughed faintly.

"Well," she said. "Never mind. Did you enjoy it?" She gestured toward the semicircle and piano.

"Yes," I said immediately. Although, I thought, I hadn't liked it, no, or rather—

"Can you believe that they'd put this on right in front of the Children's Wing?" said Kirstie.

"I'm sorry?"

"The *Kindertotenlieder*," she said, shaking her head. She

spoke as though the word were the whole of the reason. "There must have been some kind of clerical error."

"I'm sorry," I said again, coldly. "I don't know what you are referencing."

"Oh," she said. "The *Kindertotenlieder* . . . You know what it means, don't you?"

I stared at her.

"Yes," I said eventually. "Well—"

I stood up to indicate that I intended to go, but as I turned toward the aisle I saw that it was still impossible; the old man was still refusing to be carted away, and obstructing the passage. Reluctantly, I took my seat again, hoping to pass the remaining moments in silence. The entire experience from start to finish had been a disappointing one, and— But I could not continue my thought, because I became aware that Kirstie, despite my hints, had not stopped looking at me, and with an intensity that had grown increasingly bizarre, as if something she read in my face warranted a thorough investigation. Her eyes had a moist look to them now, and I noticed for the first time that they were red-rimmed at the edges. If I had not known better, I would have said that she had been crying, or, worse, that she was about to cry.

I cleared my throat once, hoping it might rouse her, but her expression did not change. It was as if she hadn't heard.

Just when I was about to make some meaningless remark, if only to break the silence, she said, in a quiet voice, lower-pitched than before, "I'm sorry, it's just—I guess I've never noticed it before."

"Noticed what?" I said.

"How much you look like him," she said, with a faraway quality in her voice. "I guess . . ." she began, and trailed off.

When I spoke I had the impression that I heard my own voice very distinctly, as though all the other sounds in the busy hospital had dropped away.

"Like whom?" I asked.

Kirstie's big eyes flicked up to meet mine, wondering, as if the answer should have been obvious. A long moment went by in which she struggled to find an answer.

"Like . . . him," she said finally, her voice dropping to a whisper. "Like your dad."

When at last I had made my way back to my office, the phone on my desk was ringing. "Hello?" I said cautiously.

"Hello," came Gerry Van Gelder's booming voice.

"Gerry," I said.

"Listen," he said. "Just wanted to give you the heads-up for tonight. Ann's father won't be able to make it, so you can come anytime after seven."

Tonight, I thought. *Tonight?*

"Oh yes," I said, automatically. "I see."

Had I agreed to have dinner with the Van Gelders that night? It was unwelcome news. But to question it now, I knew, would have been fruitless. Gerry had a force of personality that brooked no protest.

"Excellent," he said. "Looking forward to this."

Well, I thought, as I hung up the phone, what a week for it. For so long my days had been marked chiefly by their solitariness, and now this.

I went to the window, pulled up the blinds, and looked down at the parking lot, where an unforgiving midday sun illuminated every crack and wrinkle in the asphalt. A tall, slender young man walked his bicycle along the path.

No joggers now, I thought absentmindedly, my cheek resting gently on the glass, thinking of how odd it had been to see Kirstie dressed in her skirt and blouse. I turned the image over in my head a few times, until it became necessary to admit something to myself, something of which I was not proud. But the fact of the matter was inescapable: I *had* seen Kirstie waving to me when I'd arrived at the rotunda, several minutes after the lunchtime concert had begun. She'd been impossible to miss, with her palm in the air, the effort causing the ruffle on her blouse to jiggle slightly, her lips forming words I couldn't hear. So why had I pretended (and so adamantly!) not to have seen her?

9 Several hours later I found myself at the Van Gelders' front door, a plastic bag of frozen profiteroles from the supermarket hanging from my left hand, my right fist poised to knock.

Here we are again, I thought. Above me the sky was just deepening into dusk, and the sticky sweet scent of night jasmine, still exotic to me after all these years, was on the air in every inhalation. So many years of coming over for dinner, I thought. So many years without any indication that anyone was enjoying it.

My knock brought not Ann nor Gerry to the door but their only child, Stephanie Van Gelder, an ungainly person who had her father's height and coloring, and who came to the door in shorts, a T-shirt, and thick white cotton socks.

"Hello, Stephanie," I said, cringing at the sound of my own voice, which was full of the false bravado I inevitably found myself employing around children.

"Hi," she said, evidently feeling no obligation to match my enthusiasm. She looked out into the evening behind me, scrutinizing the empty street as if it might reveal a more interesting dinner guest.

I had stepped around her into the dimly lit house and sat to remove my shoes in the foyer when the most obese of the three

Van Gelder cats, a black, dandruffy creature, padded silently into the living room and noticed my arrival. He changed course, adjusting his leisurely pace not a hair, and when he reached me he began to wind in figure eights around my ankles. I gave him a long, slow stroke, and felt the wiggle of warm skin under fur.

"Mmm, profiteroles!" said Ann Van Gelder, appearing and bending to give me a quick, dry kiss on the cheek. "Gerry's in the garage."

She had always been a plain, mousey-looking woman, even in the first flush of youth, though tonight she was looking particularly colorless, and she had had her hair cut in a new way. It was difficult to put a finger on how *exactly* it was different, but whatever the change was, it had made everything a little worse: more severe, exposing new swaths of neck that looked unaccustomed to the light.

"Is that a new haircut?" I said, rising from the bench and handing over the profiteroles.

"Yes, actually," she said, sounding surprised and gratified. She gave the nape of her neck a quick, involuntary caress. "You're the first to notice."

How unlucky, I thought. That would teach me a lesson.

Ann and Gerry had been my neighbors when I first came to the university many years ago. My father had secured me a place in graduate student housing, though I was not a graduate student, and theirs was the apartment opposite my own. Since then we had remained friends, although in the last decade the friendship had calcified into this arrangement: every couple of months or so a dinner invitation would be issued, and I would appear, and no sooner had I stepped across their threshold than time would slow to a barely perceptible crawl. The only sign that the years were passing at all was in Stephanie, who had begun life as a cheerful thing, the mistress of a terrarium of salamanders, but who had recently morphed into an unpleasant and sullen-looking adolescent who, when she got her way, ate her dinner in her room.

Still, I thought, as I followed Ann into the kitchen and watched her put the profiteroles in the refrigerator to defrost, I suppose you could also say that in some sense the Van Gelders were my closest friends.

"Gerry just got back from North Dakota," said Ann, as we sat down to eat: a salad, a poached fish, green beans, a warm roll each, and a stick of yellow margarine in the butter dish.

"I see," I said. "And how was that?"

Gerry took a bite of roll and a gulp of wine and shook his head. "To tell you the truth," he said, "it's very bleak."

"Oh?"

"Just flat and ugly, and as far as the eye can see."

I made an appreciative noise. I noticed a bowl of new potatoes, split one open on my plate, nestled a yellow square of margarine in it, and reached for the salt.

"The chair of the department did his postdoc out here, actually," said Gerry. "Swedish guy. A giant. Claims there's just one thing that he really misses about California."

And after his significant pause Ann asked patiently, "And what was that?"

Gerry leaned back in his chair and pointed what remained of his roll at us.

"Would you two like to guess?"

We looked blankly at him.

"Sunshine," said Ann.

"Ocean," I said.

Gerry wagged his roll "no." It was clear that there was some expected rejoinder, and yet for the life of me I could not supply it. So much had recently occurred, I thought—the concert, the guest lecturer, the death of my father! I did not have the capacity for this, too.

"Any more guesses?"

But we were out.

"Produce," he said, shaking his head in amazement. "He said his kids won't stop bugging him about avocados."

It was clear that laughter was now expected, and I obliged, but the sound I produced missed the mark somehow, and I noticed that Ann had remained conspicuously silent.

Now she briskly margarined her own roll. "Well," she said, casting a glance down the hallway to where, presumably, her daughter was lurking. "It's true that we are very lucky in many ways, living in California, though personally I have never understood the big fuss about avocados. Don't forget to call the hotel about the bag," she added, as she rose from her seat. "Excuse me, I'm going to go make Stephanie a plate."

When she had disappeared into the kitchen Gerry turned to me and shook his head with a long-suffering expression.

"All the avocados in the world would be wasted on that woman," he said, in a lower voice. "She doesn't even like Mexican food."

I managed to produce a small, grim smile. What was it about being married to someone, I thought, that brought out these small pettinesses?

"Did you lose your bag?" I asked, without really considering what I was saying. I meant only to fill the silence, to head off any more talk with the whiff of the battlefield. Why *had* Ann been so snitty about the avocados? I wondered.

"Yes," said Gerry. Suddenly he seemed very disinterested in the conversation. "In Bismarck."

I had a sudden pang of longing for my own dinner table then, where, had the day gone differently, I could have at that very moment been sitting in peaceful silence, watching the fog roll in from the sea.

"You haven't been here since the summer, have you?" said Gerry.

I shook my head no.

"So you haven't seen the pictures from Croatia?"

I shook my head again.

"Well, we'll have to remedy that," said Gerry, with no trace of irony. "As soon as possible."

He was efficient with the projector, and soon Gerry, Ann, and I were ensconced in the living room, glasses of wine in hand, facing the hearth. The creaky old machine whirred to life, and suddenly a sparkling blue sea appeared above the mantel.

"The view from the boat," said Gerry.

Next was a vine-covered villa they'd rented, a stray cat that had been Stephanie's particular friend, a tanned and handsome waiter. Dinner had tired me, and it was a relief to observe the two-dimensional Van Gelders on the wall, accompanied by Gerry's calm drone, rather than to engage the flesh-and-blood Van Gelders in dialogue. All day I had hurried from one appointment to the next, it seemed, and now at last there was room for a breather, a little time to stop and think.

And just like that I found my attention drifting to the lunchtime concert of the *Kindertotenlieder*. What a disappointment that had been, on the musical front, at least. But Kirstie—here Gerry clicked through to a photo of Ann and Stephanie sunbathing in modest swimming suits—there was something about her that warranted looking into. That she would remark upon my resemblance to my late father was unexpected, to say the least.

Of course, given my father's position at the university, it was not implausible that Kirstie should have some familiarity with his appearance, and it was also true that there was a family resemblance. Quite a striking one, according to some. But was that a reason to look so moistly and unappealingly forlorn? The concert, perhaps, had affected her. I shook my head, forgetting I was not alone. How anyone could have paid attention to that singing long enough to be moved to tears was beyond me.

Beside me I heard the soft clink of Ann's wedding ring on her wineglass. We were seated beside each other on the sofa and she was sitting as still as a statue, shrouded in shadow. I could hear her breathing, and from time to time she made small exhalations that somehow managed to convey dissatisfaction. The more I sat and listened to them, the more I had a nagging sense that these expressions were somehow for my benefit. But, I thought, as I had that morning about the briefcase, this was only a distraction, immaterial to the investigation.

Above the mantel another seascape had appeared, a bright Dalmatian blue. On the other hand, I thought, thinking of Kirstie again, perhaps I was reading too much into it. It could simply have been an excess of emotion; women were susceptible to that, in my experience, for no reason other than biological disposition. My own mother, a highly logical person, not prone to displays of affection, had been the exception rather than the rule. And perhaps it was because I'd had her, for so long, as my only example, that I found the condition so distasteful in other women.

10 I drove home, a foil-wrapped pair of rolls and a Tupperware of cold salmon beside me in the passenger seat. I brushed my teeth, crawled into bed, switched on the lamp, and reached for my Swedish police novel, but could not quite bring myself to open it. I considered the snowscape on its cover with regret, then put it aside. As I lay in bed waiting for sleep, I had the nagging feeling that I had forgotten something, something of importance. Whatever it was had happened at the Van Gelders', but when I tried to think of all that had occurred there, I could recall nothing of interest. It was all muddled now—Gerry's routine about his trip to North Dakota, the slideshow in the living room, Ann Van Gelder talking about her haircut—I could no longer remember what fragment of conversation went with which part. Even this I cannot do, I thought with disgust. And what was more, I felt that recently I had been finding myself in this position more and more, with the unwelcome feeling that I had missed something crucial.

What was it my horoscope had said? *Now you find yourself uniquely positioned to set things in motion.* Not likely! I thought. I was more like that black bird I had seen on the lawn that morning through the bay window, scratching and scratching, but in search of what?

And now! I thought. Now I have successfully completed a metaphor: myself as bird.

Very useful! I thought bitterly. A big advance in the investigation.

Through the crack in my bedroom window I could hear the crickets' two-note chirp and, farther away, the roll and crash of the sea.

Death is just the other side of life, I thought. It follows life just as one wave follows the next. And then I thought, How ridiculous, these are like sentiments written on bookmarks; I must be exhausted. I closed my eyes and, almost immediately, fell asleep.

I dreamed I was in the hospital again, for the lunchtime concert of the *Kindertotenlieder*, only this time I was seated not next to Kirstie, but the guest lecturer. She was wearing her lavender suit jacket, and her hand was resting on my knee. I tapped her politely on the shoulder and said, "Excuse me, but would you mind taking your hand off my knee?"

She turned to look at me, a quick, annoyed flick of the eyes in which there was no sign of recognition.

"Shh," she said, turning her attention back to the concert. "Please be quiet."

I followed her gaze to the stage, where the pale, heavyset young man was singing, his hands clasped together and resting delicately on the shelf of his substantial belly. Somehow, I thought, she must have misunderstood. I tried to shift my leg so that her hand would fall in a natural-seeming way to the side, but every way my leg moved her palm went with it, as if it had been fixed there with glue.

"Excuse me," I whispered again, tapping her on the shoulder again. "I don't think you understand—"

The guest lecturer turned her head all the way around this time, a look of quiet ferocity in her eye that had certainly never been there in real life.

"Not now," she hissed. "This is not the right time."

"No—" I began, but she silenced me with one imperious glance.

"*You* are the one who doesn't understand," she said. "This is not the right sequence of events. *I* will get in touch with *you*."

With this, she turned back to the concert with a finality that precluded all compromise. I was, needless to say, both astonished by her response and completely unable to understand it. What did she mean about getting in touch with me? About the right sequence of events? And yet, as incomprehensible as it was, my dream-self seemed to take this development with equanimity. There wasn't much time to try to understand what she'd said, either, because no sooner had I sat back in my chair than I felt a light tap on my shoulder.

It was the dark-haired, smooth-faced young man from the reception desk at the Old Mission Hotel, the one who'd pointed out to me that my watch had stopped. The dream-me felt no surprise at seeing him there, in the hospital; I accepted it as a matter of course. He looked exactly as he had when I'd last seen him, down to the shine on his black lace-up shoes, and in manner seemed as crisp and poised as ever.

"Excuse me, sir," he said. "Someone is waiting for you upstairs."

Like the guest lecturer's, his lips didn't move as he spoke, and yet I heard every word clearly.

"Upstairs?" I mouthed, and looked at the glass wall of the rotunda, the fountain visible behind the singing man, white water arcing against blue sky. And as I did so, the hospital, the guest lecturer, the concert all fell away, and the dark-haired young man and I were in the elevator of the hotel, riding up to the fourth floor.

"Any idea who asked for me?" I said. I was pleased; my words had come out in a very relaxed way—it felt like a natural question to have asked.

"I'm sorry," said the young man, and shook his head.

Just then the elevator came to a stop, and the doors opened, and the young man inclined his head in a slightly different way, a way that was clearly meant to indicate: *After you*.

I stepped out into the darkened hallway, which was in every respect just as it had been in waking life: dark, with dark red wallpaper, the thick carpet soft and pillowy underfoot. I walked down it until I came to the door of Room 409, where I hung back for a moment, hesitating.

"You're certain they're expecting me?" I asked. But there was no reply. When I turned around I saw that I was alone in the hallway—the dark-haired young man had vanished.

But this, too, was not too daunting an obstacle for the dream version of myself, who, it appeared, was much better at taking things in stride than I was in real life. I turned back to the door, ready to knock, and saw that there was no need, because it was now ajar.

"Hello?" I called.

From inside the room, there was no answer. I pushed the door open and went inside.

At first glance, the room was empty. Everything was just as it had been before. The bed, the desk, the thick ocher curtain. In my dream I was able to examine several places at once. I looked at the bed. It had been made. But then again, I thought, a bed is easily made and unmade. And then I thought, Christ almighty! Even in my dreams I cannot escape these ridiculous thoughts.

The briefcase, I thought. Time in the dream seemed to be speeding up, such that the moment I thought the words "the briefcase," I was kneeling before the desk, my hand groping in the dark recess beneath. Half a second later the gold buckles flashed, and the briefcase lay open on my lap. It was empty.

How odd, I thought. The last time I was here things were very different. And then I thought, Perhaps this is a different briefcase. But before I could think that thought through to its logical conclusion, before I could even begin to think it, I became aware of another new development—something else that was different about this dream version of the hotel room, which I had failed to notice upon entering: the sound of running water, coming from the direction of the bathroom.

I laid the briefcase down carefully on the floor and listened. It was the sound of someone drawing a bath. It had escaped my attention somehow that the door to the bathroom was ajar, and the light was on inside, and a long illuminated strip lay across the carpet.

"I wouldn't go in there if I were you," said a female voice. I turned.

Kirstie was sitting on the edge of the bed, dressed in her usual shiny black athletic clothing. In my dream her presence seemed perfectly natural.

"Why not?" I asked.

Kirstie looked down at her feet, as if deciding what to say. "There's something in the bathtub."

"What?"

She shook her head. "I wouldn't go in there if I were you," she repeated.

I nodded. None of that was particularly helpful, and I had my own question to ask.

"The last time I was here," I began, "there was something in this briefcase."

Kirstie looked at the briefcase and shuddered. Then, collecting herself, she said, "That's right. There was something. It's been moved."

"Moved where?" I asked.

She closed her eyes. When she spoke again it was in a thick, dreamy voice, quite unlike her own.

"It's on its way back here."

"But where is it now?"

The water in the bathroom was rushing loudly now, so that I had to raise my voice to be heard above it.

"What did you say?" said Kirstie.

"Where is it now?" I practically shouted, over the sound of the veritable waterfall coming from the bathroom.

Suddenly the room was pitch-black, I could see nothing, and I was sitting on the bed alongside Kirstie, a fact that I knew only because I could hear her breathing very close to me. These developments made the thread of the conversation even harder to follow.

"It's where you'll find it," Kirstie whispered.

"But where will I find it?"

But though I meant to speak the words, I had the impression that I had not, in fact, said anything at all, that though I had opened my mouth and moved my lips, no sound had emerged. The darkness was thick all around us, pressing in, as if all the air had been sucked out of the room, and the only living thing in it was the heat of Kirstie's breath, its quick inhale-exhale caressing my skin. More and more I was convinced that I had not succeeded in asking my last question, and I was just about to try to ask it again when I was startled—genuinely startled—by the sound of applause.

11 I woke, wide-eyed, and sat up in bed. Nearby, some unseen time-keeping device ticked inexorably. What a peculiar dream, I thought, and then, a little later: What an admirable synthesis of all that has recently passed. Eventually, I lay down again and closed my eyes, but I slept only fitfully and woke before dawn, when I rose and ate breakfast in the dark.

I had been sitting at the table with my toast and coffee, my thoughts still full of my dream, when I realized that it was Saturday. The whole day stretched out before me, as unpeopled as a prairie in winter.

But, I thought now, there is no reason to feel that way on this weekend of all weekends, because there *is* work to be done, work on the investigation into your father's death, and what could be more worthwhile than that?

I got up, poured myself a second cup of coffee, and retrieved a pen and the notebook I kept by the telephone for messages. Not, presumably, how actual investigators did things, but I would make do.

First, I thought, begin at the beginning. That was the open house, where I'd found the stationery with the drawing of the steeple. Then the dinner with the guest lecturer, and my brief, unplanned visit to the Old Mission Hotel. The next day, the lunchtime concert of the *Kindertotenlieder*, where I'd seated myself next to Kirstie, and she had commented on my physical resemblance to my father. Then, that evening—yesterday evening, I amended—dinner with the Van Gelders, and in the night, my dream, in which Kirstie and the guest lecturer had both featured, although in my dream, I noted, their roles had been reversed: Kirstie had been at the Old Mission Hotel, and the guest lecturer at the concert.

I looked up at the bay window for a moment. Could this all have really happened in the course of a few days? Certainly, events seemed to be building on themselves at a rate I had not personally experienced before.

But that was enough marveling at events, I told myself. I could use the day to decide how to proceed. First I considered the open house: Would it be helpful to return? I sipped my coffee and thought. No, I concluded. The real estate agent had already been there, confusing the situation with her props and scents—it had been a stroke of pure luck that I had found the stationery there. The guest lecturer, too, I dismissed, despite the grotesque thing in the briefcase and her strange prominence in my dream. She was nothing but a distraction; the reason being: she had nothing to do with my father.

Two possible avenues presented themselves. First, there was Kirstie's declaration at the lunchtime concert of the *Kindertotenlieder*. True, it was not exactly incriminating to say I resembled my father; to be sure, anyone could have said it. But as I had conjectured on the Van Gelders' sofa, it was also possible that there was something more there, some depth to be plumbed. Still, the more I turned things over in my mind, the more convinced I became that my second idea would be more fruitful: to return to the Old Mission Hotel. People were changeable, I thought; there was no telling what they might say if they thought it suited them. But a place held all its history without bias, like layers that sat one on top of the other. It could no more hide or delete them than a leopard could change its spots.

I took another sip of coffee. But how to return?

The answer did not come to me until Monday afternoon. I had slept poorly the night before (poorly but without dreams), and as I crossed the reservoir that morning, coming out from under the thick of the ridge, I could see that the black sky was beginning to purple at the edges; dawn would break soon. I thought to myself: So this will be one of those days, long and disconnected, made mournful by lack of sleep.

In the afternoon I began to feel the effects more acutely; words were beginning to blur together, to require rereading once, twice, then three times. I took myself back to the break room for another cup of coffee.

I had barely flipped the switch to warm the pot when the thought came to me, fully formed. Of course, I thought, of course! I brought my hand down triumphantly on the counter, causing a selection of teas to jump. I had the piece of information on which my thoughts had snagged, which I had tried and failed to remember that night after dinner. It was, of all things, what Gerry Van Gelder had said about his trip to North Dakota—or rather, it was Ann's rejoinder: "Don't forget to call the hotel about the bag," she had said, as if it confirmed what she had suspected for years about Gerry and bags, that he was incapable of remembering them. Stop, I told myself, that is exactly the kind of thinking you don't want. The salient thing was that people left their belongings behind sometimes, at hotels, and then they called to retrieve them. It was a usual, natural thing, something people did every day. Or if not exactly every day, then commonly. And I could do it, too. Not exactly like Gerry, of course, because I had no reason to believe that my father had left a bag at the Old Mission Hotel, but I could at least discover if he'd stayed there at all. Because it had occurred to me that a piece of hotel stationery might end up in one's coat pocket for any number of reasons. There was at any rate *something* to be gained, I was sure of it. With two fingers, I felt the coffeepot—it was still tepid. But perhaps I didn't need coffee at all, I decided, and strode out into the hall with new vigor.

Back in my office I retrieved the phone book from the shelf above my desk, and within moments I had located the number and placed the call. Someone picked up on the first ring, but before speaking gave a tiny but noticeable space, like the time one might leave for throat-clearing.

"This is the Old Mission Hotel," said a male voice, and I was almost certain that it was the smooth-faced young man who had pointed out that my watch had stopped, and who had appeared in my dream.

"Hello," I said, and I felt a certain facility with words, not unlike the one imagined in my dream. "I'm calling about a bag I left behind."

"I'd be happy to help you with that, sir," said the young man. "You were a guest at the hotel?"

"Yes," I said. How simple this was, I thought, what a breeze. *I was a guest at the hotel.* This is how an investigation is performed, no doubt about it.

"What were the dates of your stay?"

"I'm sorry?"

There was another pause. "The dates of your stay, sir?"

Suddenly all my triumphant thoughts came to a hasty halt.

"The dates of my stay," I murmured, when too long a silence had elapsed. Of course, how could I have been so stupid?

"I'm sorry," I said. "I don't remember them."

There was a little silence on the other end—not impolite, but patient.

"I'm sorry," I said again, making an effort to sound careless and blithe, although the palm I had pressed to the phone had grown unhelpfully damp. "It would have been in the last six months or so."

Another little pause.

"I travel quite frequently," I said unhappily.

"I see," said the young man. Still he did not sound the least bit annoyed. I began to take heart; perhaps this was a normal occurrence.

"Perhaps it would be easier to look you up by name instead," he said.

"Yes," I said immediately. "Yes, of course. My name is . . ." and, surprised at how natural it felt, I spelled my father's name.

"Thank you," said the young man. "Just a moment."

I heard the soft sound of the phone being put down on the desk. Then, more faintly, I heard the sound of music playing in the lobby, just as it had been on the night I'd walked through it with the guest lecturer. I pictured her waving coquettishly, with just the tips of her fingers, at the smooth-faced young man. How unfortunate that had been. I pictured the long bar with its row of candles and, on the far side of the room, the low white curving couches. Was the lobby empty now? I wiped the perspiration from my palm on the leg of my pants, and switched the phone to my other ear.

"Hello?" said the young man.

"Yes?" I said.

"Could the reservation have been made under another name, sir?"

Another name? I thought. Another name? Of course, it could have been, but if I knew it I would be considerably further along in my investigation than I was, or perhaps ever would be.

"No," I said, trying to keep the disappointment from my voice. "I don't think it could be."

"I see," said the man. "I'm sorry, but I don't appear to have any record of your stay."

I cleared my throat. "How odd. Well, it's possible it's been longer than six months . . ." I trailed off.

"Yes, I thought of that," said the young man. "It's an un-usual name, so I was able to go through the records from the last year without too much trouble. We don't have any record of your stay here from that time.

"I'm sorry, sir. We do have a lost-and-found closet—if you'd like to give me a description of the bag, I can check, just in case."

A description of the bag, I thought. But of course there

was no bag. Because my father had not left a bag at the hotel. Because, in fact, he had never stayed there at all.

"No, thank you," I said. "That's all right. I must be mistaken."

Perhaps it just wasn't meant to be, I thought, as I set a pot of water on the stove at home that evening. True, I had not expected my investigation of my father's death to come to such an unceremonious end, but the more I thought about it, the more it occurred to me that it was likely that there were two kinds of people: those who exerted a force on the world, who influenced events, who shaped outcomes by the sheer power of their wills, and those who did not.

I took a packet of bacon out of the freezer and put a few pieces in a pan to fry. Was it really that surprising, I thought, to discover I was in the latter camp?

My father, he had been one of those who could set things in motion; he had that quality. If only *he* were investigating his *own* death, I thought, and then I laughed once, startling myself in the silence of the kitchen. The water was boiling now, and I added salt and then spaghetti. I poured a jar of tomato sauce into a pan. Everything had gone wrong, really, almost everything.

Then another thought wriggled its way up: Was it really so bad?

If, I thought, as I excised a sage-green crust of mold from a wedge of parmesan, the hotel had confirmed the fact that my father had stayed there, what would I have done? I was not a member of the police force, I could not have appeared on the scene to interrogate the personnel, and that was not even accounting for the fact that most likely they would not have remembered him at all. This was not television, it was real life, and deaths did not divulge clues at regular intervals. I drained the pasta in the colander, stirred the sauce, grated the cheese over it, and sat myself down in the chair facing the bay window. The sky was a familiar white gray, and I could see, just barely, that the fog had gathered, as if in anticipation, above the waterline. And was this, I thought again, really so bad? To eat a humble but well-cooked meal in the comfort of one's home?

Sometimes it is acceptable to admit defeat.

After dinner I washed my dishes, showered, and climbed into bed with my book. It had been a few days since I had picked it up—since, I marveled, the night of the open house. I had missed it, and I soon found myself happily engrossed in the universe of semirural Sweden, where temperatures had fallen below zero, and the murder victim's brother had just come forward with a surprising story about an illegitimate child. Our detective is dubious, but he also has other things on his mind. He is about to have dinner with his ex-wife, for whom he still carries a torch. They are to meet in a real restaurant, and for the occasion the secretary of his department has had his suit dry-cleaned. I knew, without even reading the rest of the chapter, how the story would unfold; in fact, I could have written it myself. His heart would skip a beat when he first caught sight of her. Candlelight would flatter her familiar features. With hope in his heart he would order a bottle of wine. She would be kind, even solicitous, urging him to eat more healthily, to watch his smoking and drinking, but finally, with a note of regret, she would announce her engagement to her current boyfriend, someone more stable, who worked regular hours, like a lawyer or a financier.

 I woke to the sound of the phone ringing in the kitchen. I struggled out of bed and felt my way nearsightedly down the hallway.

From the look of the sky, or what I could see of it, dawn had just broken. I sighed inwardly—at this early hour it was most likely to be a wrong number.

Still, I had already made it this far, so I picked up the receiver and said hello.

"Hello," said a female voice. "How are you this morning?"

"Oh," I said. "No, thank you. I'm not interested."

The caller did not respond, and I thought to myself that I should hang up immediately, but some misplaced sense of decorum made me stay on the line, waiting.

"Hang on," said the caller. "I'm not selling anything. Don't you recognize my voice?"

And strangely enough, I did. Or I thought I did. I had not had that sense to begin with, but now that she mentioned it, on second thought, yes, there *was* something familiar about her voice.

"I do," I said. My mind, still half asleep, was having difficulty putting everything in the correct order. Without my glasses, the view from the window was a blurred grayish green.

"I do recognize your voice, somehow, and yet I'm having some trouble placing you . . . Who is this?"

"Who I am is not important," she said. "I have some information you need."

For a second I had been fooled into thinking the voice sounded familiar, but in the end it was just a telemarketer, employing a needlessly complicated scheme aimed at confusing people who were not yet fully awake.

"No, thank you," I said. "There isn't any information I need."

Again I thought, why not just hang up now, and be done with it? But this was an ability I did not have. And never would have, come to think of it. I was not assertive. Surely the Swedish detective in my novel, for all his faults, would have hung up the phone long ago.

"Are you sure about that?" said the woman mildly. Really, I thought, these people were unbelievably dogged. Then she said, "It's about your father."

I must have misheard, was my first thought. When you have a hammer, I thought, everything looks like a nail. And yet when I spoke again I felt a dryness in my throat that had not been there before.

"I'm sorry," I was finally able to say, swallowing for moisture. "What did you say?"

"You heard me correctly," said the woman. "Meet me in the Arboretum at noon today and I will give you the information you need."

"In the Arboretum . . ." I trailed off. "But how will I recognize you?"

If I'd had to guess merely from her voice I would have said my caller was anywhere from thirty to fifty years of age, and

American—there could be dozens of women meeting that description in the Arboretum at any given time.

"Oh," she said. "Don't worry about that."

There was the shadow of a chuckle in her voice. "You'll recognize me. We've met before."

13 It was not accurate, I saw at once, when at five minutes before noon I crossed the road and entered the Arboretum, to say that there could have been dozens of American women from thirty to fifty years of age there at any given time. As far as I could see, there were no women in the grove of trees except one, and she was watching over a group of school-age children who were hitting the ground with sticks at the base of a low-spreading oak. This woman did not seem right at all: she was too young, she was dressed in hiking clothing, accompanied by a male counterpart, and did not so much as glance in my direction as I passed by. She was not my mysterious caller, I was sure of it. And not only were there no other women in the Arboretum, there was no one else of any gender in my line of sight.

And yet, I thought, as I surveyed the horizon line of mature trees against the blue sky, it was true that the nature of a grove of trees is such that it is not really possible to see all its angles at once. I would walk around for a while, I decided, before abandoning the enterprise altogether, and for the second time that day I thought of the Swedish policeman in the novel I was reading, and how he might have handled the situation. It seemed unlikely that he would have found himself in exactly this predicament, I thought, as I set off on a dirt path that curved away from campus. I could not pinpoint exactly how, though I had the general sense that he would have found it undignified to traipse around the Arboretum in search of an anonymous female caller. The weather, for one thing, I thought a moment later, as I felt the back of my neck grow moist with perspiration, was all wrong. The Swedish detective, who was perpetually strapping on his overcoat, whose car thermometer was routinely dropping five, now ten, now fifteen degrees below zero—surely he would have been at a loss here, under these preternaturally blue skies, in this balmy breeze, on which wafted the slightly mentholated fragrance of eucalyptus.

A fat, speckled squirrel was watching me from a drainage ditch. It was a little surprising, I thought, as I stopped to return his beady stare, that I had never been compelled to walk in the Arboretum before. Really, it was very pleasant. Beside me a stand of green foxtails waved ever so slightly, and in the distance there was a shallow pond from the depths of which tall grasses emerged like the heads of spears. And there—I stopped. Because next to the shallow pond was a bench, and on the bench was, I was almost certain, the woman who had telephoned me early that morning, purporting to have news of my father. She seemed to be, as I had suspected, Caucasian and middle-aged, and beyond that I could not say anything more, because she was sitting with her back to me and wearing a wide-brimmed, cream-colored hat that completely obscured the back of her head.

Or, I thought, as I quickly covered the distance between the path and the bench, it was not *news* of my father that she'd claimed to have, exactly, but—what were the words she'd used?—*information I needed* about him.

"Excuse me," I said, as I approached the bench. There was a slightly hysterical note in my voice, I noticed at once with some displeasure. I did my best to tamp it down.

"Excuse me," I said again, in a lower register. I wiped a sudden moisture from my palms on the legs of my pants.

Just when I thought that the woman seemed strangely immobile, like she hadn't heard me at all, I saw her right hand dart out and pat the bench beside her.

"Come and sit down," I heard her say. It was the same voice I'd heard on the telephone that day: slow, calm, and now uncannily disembodied behind that large white hat. Gingerly, I walked around the side of the bench and sat down beside her. For no particular reason I kept my eyes staring straight ahead, as though I were seating myself next to a large and dangerous animal unfond of eye contact. I saw before me the little pond, and the dirt path beyond it. A very old eucalyptus was directly in our view, its bark peeling off in long strips.

I became aware that the woman beside me on the bench was wearing perfume, and in the same moment I knew that it was not the first time that I had smelled this particular perfume. I turned to look at her—and a curious sensation passed through my body, as though all the blood in my veins had been momentarily replaced with ice water, and then just as quickly restored.

Sitting beside me on the bench was the guest lecturer. The very same guest lecturer whom I'd accompanied to the Old Mission Hotel on Thursday of the previous week. The lavender suit jacket was gone now, and in its place was a cream-colored linen suit. On her feet, she was wearing a pair of sandals that appeared to be made of straw.

"You see?" she said. "I told you you'd recognize me."

"Yes," I said.

A silence passed in which she seemed to be waiting for me to speak. "I'm sorry," I said eventually. "I'm not sure I understand."

The guest lecturer smiled indifferently and gave her hat a slight adjustment. Evidently, if she planned to explain anything, she was not prepared to do it yet.

"I was under the impression that your flight home was on Friday evening."

It was not what I had wanted to say at all, it missed the point entirely, and yet, it did not seem to matter very much in the end, because the guest lecturer showed no signs that she was going to answer. Instead, she merely sat and regarded me with a slightly smug expression.

It occurred to me just then that it might be helpful to remember what the guest lecturer's real name was, although now, conveniently, any inkling of it had completely vanished from my mind. I had known it at one point, I was sure of that. Carol? I thought. Alicia?

"Amanda," said the guest lecturer suddenly. "Amanda Payard was the name I gave you." I looked at her, stunned. Was she, in addition to being a guest lecturer, an academic from Colorado, a maker of anonymous phone calls, also a reader of minds?

"But that name is not important now," she went on.

I swallowed, and nodded.

"Listen," said the guest lecturer, with an air that suggested that the preliminary portion of the conversation was now coming to a close. "I'm here to help you."

I nodded again.

"But I don't have very much time. You're going to have to listen very carefully to what I have to say. Can you do that?"

I had the fleeting thought that this guest lecturer, although physically identical to the one I'd met before, had an entirely different manner.

"Yes," I said. "Yes, of course."

"Good," she said. She adjusted the crease of her linen pants.

"I understand," she said, "that you are in the midst of an investigation into your father's death."

I nodded, temporarily unable to speak. To hear one's secret projects spoken aloud by someone else—I was deeply moved. But there was no time to think of that now, because the guest lecturer had already begun to speak again.

"That's good," she said. "It's admirable."

She went on: "It has come to my attention that you attempted to make inquiries at the Old Mission Hotel, concerning whether or not your father had been a guest there."

She turned to look at me with her eyebrows raised.

"That's right," I said hoarsely.

"That was also good," she said. "You're on the right track."

I heard myself whisper faintly, "On the right track?"

"Yes," said the guest lecturer. "But here's the thing," she said, and her voice took on a new, more serious note. "That isn't the right name."

"Not the right name?" I repeated. I was having trouble keeping everything straight.

"No," said the guest lecturer, and now she was the picture of seriousness. "You need to ask about a different name."

I swallowed.

"Are you saying," I said, feeling a little feverish, "that my father stayed at the hotel under an alias?"

It had not occurred to me, and yet it was so simple. Of course, when people want to cover their tracks, they use false names.

The guest lecturer gave me a withering look. "Yes," she said. "That's exactly what I mean."

At this juncture in the meeting she lifted her wrist to look at a small silver watch—had she worn it the night we'd met? It did not look familiar—and frowned.

I wanted to tell her to wait, that I didn't yet understand what she was saying, but before I could do so I was interrupted by the sight of something that struck me as odd.

From her left wrist to her left elbow stretched a long, thin scar—when she'd raised her arm to look at her watch, the sleeve of her jacket had fallen down, exposing it. This was no trick of the light; I could see the seam of tissue clearly, a slightly raised, shiny white scar.

"This is the information you need," said the guest lecturer, interrupting my thoughts. She produced a folded piece of notepaper, which she held out for me to take. This particular size and shape of notepaper were at this point very familiar to me.

The questions I had—how did she come by that scar? what was her interest in my investigation?—began to tumble into one another; I had so many that in the end they seemed to cancel each other out. I noticed that sitting on the bench on the other side of the guest lecturer was a handbag made of the same straw-like material as her shoes.

I looked down at the folded piece of paper in my hand.

"Will I see you again?" I said, and then I thought, Well, that strikes the wrong tone, how needlessly romantic and strained.

The guest lecturer thought a moment, her head cocked to one side. She gave me a long, appraising look that seemed to end in disappointment.

"Yes," she said finally. "I expect you will."

I did my best to look pleased.

"It's possible," she went on, "that you might be able to accomplish everything on your own, but . . ." She shrugged slowly. "My guess is that yes, we will meet again."

I nodded. I had, of course, not the faintest idea what she was talking about.

With that the guest lecturer brushed off the legs of her pants, picked up her straw handbag, and stood up from the bench, steadying her hat with one hand as she rose. The sharp vertical creases that had been ironed into each of her pant legs fell into place, like the prows of two identical ships.

"Wait," I said, with a sudden flash of inspiration. "Do you know who MC is? MC, Saturday, ten a.m.?"

The guest lecturer looked down at me, a stern expression on her face.

"It's not a person," she said. "It's a place."

She seemed to be on the verge of leaving.

"Wait," I said again. "Can you tell me anything else?"

"No," she said. "I can't."

I nodded dumbly.

"Well," she said. "It's been a pleasure." Her tone suggested that the opposite was true. "Now you'll have to excuse me."

I would have liked to turn and watch her go—how had she

arrived? was one question I had. On foot? By car? But to do so seemed somehow unbecoming, so instead I kept my eyes trained on the shallow pond in front of me, and I listened for the brisk crunch of each footstep on the path until I heard them no more. Cautiously, I turned my head. She was gone.

I walked back to my office, tracing a roughly diagonal line across campus. By the time I'd reached the front door of my building I was incredibly thirsty and could feel a scrim of dried perspiration on the back of my neck. I had already, of course, read what was written on the piece of folded paper that the guest lecturer had given me—it was the first thing I had done while still sitting on the bench, following her departure.

My suspicion had been correct—it was a piece of stationery from the Old Mission Hotel. That, in and of itself, however, was unremarkable, I told myself, because that was where the guest lecturer had stayed; I'd seen her in her hotel room with my own eyes! No doubt the explanation was simply that it had been the most convenient piece of notepaper at her disposal. I shook my head. The fact that the guest lecturer had written her note to me on the hotel stationery with which I'd recently become so intimately familiar was the least remarkable development in the whole series of recent events.

Considerably less remarkable, for example, than the scar on her arm. It had not escaped my notice that it was a scar the shape and orientation of which I had seen before, on the real estate agent's arm at my father's open house. A coincidence, surely, but what were the odds? A connection between the two women seemed unlikely at best.

Then I came to what was written on the piece of paper—a name, just as she'd promised: Daniel Shriver—a name with absolutely no significance for me. Nor, to my knowledge, was it connected in any way to my father. Though it was true that I was far from having a complete list of his contacts. And when people used aliases to check into hotel rooms (something I had no experience with myself) did they necessarily use names of personal significance? Surely sometimes it was more convenient to invent one out of thin air, or to pluck one at random from a newspaper or a film. Daniel Shriver—it could be someone, or no one at all.

I took the elevator up to the second floor and went to the break room for a glass of water, then sat down at the round plastic table to catch my breath. Someone had left a red-and-yellow box of candy on the table, and absentmindedly I pulled it toward me. A note taped to the lid of the box read simply, *Enjoy!* —*PP*. My whirring thoughts stuttered and went still. PP, I thought. Professor Pindar. So he was back, I thought unhappily. I had pushed the box away from me and now I brought it close again, because I wanted to give it another look. *Dulce de Tamarindo*, it said in big yellow letters. I opened the box—inside it was filled with petite red sugar-covered patties, each in its own frilly paper cup.

Of course, I thought, he has been in Mexico on vacation, and this is evidently some kind of local food he has retrieved. Nothing to be concerned about, I told myself. My mind flitted unhelpfully to the events of the other night, and I realized I would have to be more specific with myself, because so many of my nights had recently been notable—I tightened my grip here on my train of thought—the night I meant was *Thurs-*

day night—the night of the dinner with the guest lecturer, and with my colleagues.

But, I told myself, and I could feel my pulse quickening, there was nothing wrong with driving an intoxicated woman to her hotel, and what was more, it was not so remarkable that anyone would feel the need to mention it to Professor Pindar. I took a swallow of water, although it seemed to have no effect on my suddenly parched throat. Well, well, I thought, grimacing, perhaps the lady doth protest too much.

15

The sun was sparkling on the reservoir as I drove home over the bridge, all the while pretending in my mind a cordial conversation. Yes, hello, this is—I pulled the piece of paper from my pocket and spread it flat against the steering wheel—Daniel Shriver. Yes, hello, this is Daniel Shriver; I'm calling about a bag I may have left in your hotel. I'm afraid I can't say for certain, sometime in the last six months or so; I travel frequently.

My mind skipped several steps ahead. This conversation—the actual future one, not the imagined one I was having in the privacy of my own vehicle—seemed suddenly pressing; who knew how long this facility with words would last? I had a vision of myself pulling over at the gas station to use the pay phone, because this *was* an investigation, I was sure of it. No minute wasted, no stone unturned. All my life I had hung back, stewing ineffectually, and here, finally, was my chance to act.

Now I had come to the end of the water and up through the thicket of pines on the ridge. The sunlight, filtered through their tall canopy, took on a sickly, greenish cast. Suddenly and unaccountably I was deflated; a gust of despair moved through me. Did anything I had just thought or said make any sense at all?

Was it at all plausible that "Daniel Shriver" had lost a bag

and yet had no idea when, and had just now set about retriev-
ing it, and in such a lackadaisical fashion? Surely people who
left their luggage behind did not wait six months to inquire
about it. The premise of luggage was that it contained items of
vital importance—the bare necessities needed to sustain oneself while traveling. It was not like leaving a superfluous item,
like a scarf or an umbrella.

But what ridiculous thoughts were these? A disquisition on
the nature of luggage? What's more, I admonished myself, it
behooved me to remember that there was no bag. There was
nothing to suggest that my father had left a bag behind; this
was only a stratagem, inspired by Gerry Van Gelder and *his*
missing bag, that I had invented in order to find out whether
or not my father had in fact been a guest at the Old Mission
Hotel.

And yet, doubt overcame me at every turn—was it truly the
most advisable way to proceed? Suddenly the whole enterprise
seemed riddled with holes. It was better to wait, I thought,
until a new scheme presented itself.

I had leftover spaghetti for dinner and drank a glass of water
at the sink. The sun had already set, and a thick, damp darkness had settled on the land.

There was one small thing I could do, I thought, and I
walked to the counter where the telephone sat and extracted
the aged phone book from the cabinet below. I saw at once
that it was several years out of date. Odd, I thought, because
I had the impression that they delivered the new ones relentlessly, but where those had disappeared to was anyone's guess.

I opened it up and thumbed through its thin pages until I came to the *Ps*—Amanda Payard was the name the guest lecturer had "given" me, whatever that meant, and once she said it I remembered seeing it printed on a name tag among her things, P-A-Y-A-R-D. But here in the listings—Pawson; Paxton; Pay-N-Save Market; and Paye, Harold—there was no such person. Well, I thought, perhaps she really did live in Colorado, with her husband and however many children she'd claimed to have. Although if that was the case, what was she still doing here, proposing assignations in the Arboretum?

I turned to *S*. Here at first it appeared I would have more luck: between Lloyd A. Shreves, of Burlingame, and George Shrom of San Mateo, there were two Shrivers, but neither was the one I wanted. They were Kenneth C. and Robert G., and not Daniel. Briefly I thought of turning to the *Cs*, but I remembered that the guest lecturer, a.k.a. Amanda Payard, had said that MC was not a person but a place.

Well, I thought, closing the phone book and returning it to its shelf, I had not expected to learn anything anyway. Surely real investigators did not do their work through the phone book.

Moodily, and more out of restlessness than hunger, I opened the cupboard and took out an opened bag of gingersnaps. I put a handful on a plate, poured myself a glass of milk, and removed the whole arrangement to the bedroom, where I propped myself up on pillows, balanced the plate of cookies on my chest, and began to read my book.

I could feel, distinctly, as I tried to orient myself within the pages, a whole host of competing thoughts pressing in, but I held firm. A man must rest, despite the greater project.

A storm had moved in overnight in our detective's personal corner of Sweden. A press conference had gone poorly, and someone in the police department had leaked sensitive information about the nature of the crime to the local TV news. Things on the personal front were no more promising; the young and attractive new public prosecutor had turned out to be married, and there had been no word from the ex-wife in the wake of their dinner.

It was easily recognizable to me as one of those little interludes in books like these where there was no discernible advancement in the investigation, but instead we sidle up to the detective in a quiet moment. It was a melancholic evening for him, alone in his apartment, the winter wind buffeting the windows, his only companions a bottle of whiskey and a recording of *Aida*.

The gingersnaps were stale, there was no denying it, but dipping them in milk made them softer and more palatable. When I'd finished them, and the milk, I read a few pages more, until the words began to swim before my eyes, and I turned the light off and went to sleep.

16 I did not allow myself to think of the investigation again until I was in the break room the next morning, a cup of coffee steaming in front of me. I had risen early and felt rested, and not even the sight of the red-and-yellow box of candy, haphazardly stuffed into a trash can otherwise full of empty beer bottles and a pizza box, could dampen my spirits. There would have been some kind of happy hour the night before, I deduced.

The last few days, I thought—and then I caught myself. Better to focus on the specific. To that end, something had occurred to me. I had made an error, I realized. It concerned the looking up of the names in the phone book. But before I could identify what exactly I had missed, the door to the break room swung open, and Alex Foss burst in, trailing behind him a tall, slender young man with a straw-blond mustache.

I'd heard Alex Foss, a junior faculty member, called a "rising star" in the department. Be that as it may, I found him unbearable, a big, boorish golden retriever of a man, and I felt an automatic sympathy for his companion, whom he introduced in his overloud voice as a Mr. Reinecke, visiting from Germany.

"Well, well, well," said Foss, gesturing at the trash can. "Big night last night?"

I smiled weakly.

"Didn't think you were the type."

It was just the kind of joke one could expect from Alex Foss. I ignored him, and stood to shake the younger man's hand, noting his firm grip, clear blue eyes, and friendly mien. A second ago I had been full of my own schemes, and now I was momentarily arrested—who was this?

"Just a quick tour of the medical school," Alex Foss was saying. With a swift movement of his head he indicated his companion. "He's interviewing for a fellowship. That a fresh pot?"

Mr. Reinecke was dressed far too formally for the occasion, I saw, in well-cut gray slacks, a pressed shirt, and leather shoes. He would get a shock, as I once had, when he met the senior faculty, in their blue jeans, athletic shoes, and ridiculous puffed vests. In fact, it was true that I saw something of myself in Mr. Reinecke, myself as a younger man.

"Yes," I said. "Please, have a cup."

I directed my remark at Mr. Reinecke, hoping somehow to communicate that I was sensitive to his plight, saddled as he was with such an unpleasant tour guide.

"This stuff is practically gasoline," Alex Foss was saying, as he flung open the cupboard and took out two mugs, each embossed with our institution's evergreen emblem.

"But the lounge in the hospital isn't open yet," he continued, pouring them each a cup. "That's where they keep the good stuff, the espresso machine." I would not have been surprised if he had winked.

He took a big gulp of coffee and made a show of grimacing. He knew as well as I did that the lounge to which he was referring, on the third floor of the hospital, was frequented exclusively by physicians, by custom if not by rule. Was Mr. Reinecke a physician? I wondered. He looked barely old enough to have a driver's license, but one never knew.

"Where in Germany are you from?" I asked.

Reinecke smiled, revealing a row of white, even teeth. No doubt he was grateful for someone to show a little interest, and for a break from Alex Foss's unrelenting chatter. There was something else about this Mr. Reinecke, I realized. All it took was a little animation of the features and it was obvious—the man was clearly a homosexual.

"From Tübingen."

His accent was cool and pleasant to the ear.

"Ah," I said. "Tübingen."

A little silence descended on the room just then. Alex Foss had been occupied with something in the refrigerator, but now I felt the beam of his attention wander across the room to settle, unwelcome, on me. Both men seemed to be waiting for me to respond. As for me, I desperately would have liked to make some remark, but Tübingen . . . Tübingen . . . the truth was that I had never heard of it.

"Well," I said at last. "Welcome."

Reinecke smiled, perhaps a little more perfunctorily than before. An uncategorizable noise escaped from Alex Foss, halfway between a cough and a hoot. You could always count on him for social delicacy.

I did my best to disregard him, and smiled back at Reinecke. Life is full of moments like this, I would have liked to say, moments of uncertainty, of false steps. Where there isn't time to say what one really means. It would have been preferable, infinitely preferable, if I could have said something, anything, about the city in question. But there you are, such is life, often we lack the information we need.

"Well," said Alex Foss, putting his half-full cup in the sink. "Should we hit the road?"

"Nice to meet you," said Reinecke.

And they were gone.

"I think I'd better be on my way, too," I said softly to myself, when I could hear their footsteps retreating down the hall. I washed my mug, set it to dry, and made my way out into the hallway, where sunlight streamed through the window and onto the floor in fat lemon-colored slabs. Despite the early hour, I thought, it was shaping up to be a pleasant morning.

Then I came around the corner, and my thoughts came abruptly to a halt. There, only several yards away, were Alex Foss and young Mr. Reinecke, stopped in the middle of the hallway with their backs to me. They had not noticed my arrival, I was sure, and without knowing why exactly, I retreated several steps backward, so that I was hidden from sight behind the corner.

And why, I thought, did you do that? Are you a dog, cringing to avoid a blow? Go ahead, I told myself, go on! But in spite of myself I remained firmly rooted to the spot.

Reinecke spoke first. His voice was too quiet for me to distinguish his exact words, but I could tell by his rising inflection that he had asked a question.

Had his interlocutor been anyone but Alex Foss, his voice would not have carried; I would never have heard the answer, and no one would have been the wiser. But, as it *was* Alex

Foss, I heard every word as clearly as if he had been standing next to me, speaking into my ear.

"Who?" he asked.

Reinecke answered, still inaudibly.

"That's a good question," said Foss. "I've never really been sure myself. But my impression is that he's some kind of glorified secretary."

To hear such bald words about yourself so early in the morning—it's discouraging, to say the least.

When I could be sure that the two men had gone, I continued on my way down the hallway, let myself into my office, and sat down at my desk. For some time I could do nothing but sit and stare into space. Might it be possible, I wondered, to simply pack up and leave for the day, to admit defeat, though the clock on my shelf showed it was not yet even eight o'clock in the morning? That was not a solution, I knew, although I would be lying if I said the thought was not tempting. Eventually I settled down and tried to do some work. I made a few half-hearted attempts at different projects, accomplishing nothing in particular. At around eleven-thirty I gave up for good, and took myself back to the break room to microwave the leftover spaghetti I had brought with me for lunch.

At the door I tensed a little, but it was mercifully quiet. I decanted my spaghetti into a bowl and covered it with a plate, put it in the battered microwave and pressed start. I stayed there, leaning against the counter, watching through the little frosted window as my spaghetti made its lazy revolutions, and as I did, an uncanny feeling crept over me, a peculiar set of conditions settled like a fog into every corner of my mind, and I felt as though I were having a strange, waking dream.

Only it was not a dream. It was a memory, a particularly clear one, of a visit my father had paid me when I was a young man living in Ottawa.

It was late spring, if I'm remembering correctly, but that means next to nothing in that region, and the weather was sulky and cold. In the days leading up to my father's visit it had rained relentlessly, and judging by the view from the small studio apartment I rented near campus, the day I planned to meet him would be no different. I was then a student at the Royal College of Surgeons, an impressive-sounding name for what was, in fact, a third-rate medical school. I was a student there still, at the time of my father's visit, at least technically, but several weeks earlier I had been caught cheating on an exam, and it was almost certain that I would be expelled.

I had suggested we meet for tea in a shop close to my apartment, which was on the second floor above a bakery. It was a small, careworn little place, but I liked it, and had spent many an afternoon there on my own with a book. I suppose it reminded me of home. It was not until I saw my father in the shop itself that I realized what a poor choice it had been; that he did not approve of it was plain. He was already sitting down, at a table in the corner, in his gray coat and self-consciously knotted scarf, his elbows hovering carefully an inch above the tablecloth, radiating discomfort. We were the shop's only customers, except for a lone East Asian woman seated by the window, who was holding her teacup in both hands and staring out at the drizzle of rain.

Well, I thought. So much for this.

I had been surprised—stunned, really—to hear from my father that he was en route. He was now, I'd learned, a senior-level dean, and it was this new position, I supposed, that had made him uniquely suited to involve himself in my little problem—or, as was more likely, had made him subject to a rare request from my mother.

And relations between the two of them were not traditional, either. I was my mother's only child, but not my father's. I was, as they say, "illegitimate," a kind of side project he'd embarked upon while he and my mother worked together briefly at the University of Leeds, when all the while he had been married to someone else. By the time I was in medical school I had met him only a handful of times, and only when I was a child. And yet, I thought, as we greeted each other awkwardly, in this stranger's face, undeniably, were echoes of my own. Would that, I wondered idly, be the fate of *my* hairline? Would *my* eyes acquire that hooded, turtle-y look in old age?

But here I should correct myself. My father could not reasonably have been described as "old-aged." When we met that day, he could not have been more than fifty.

We sat down across the little table, each of us doing his best not to look too closely at the other. We exchanged a few pleasantries then, about what exactly I can't remember, but the whole thing was fits and false starts until he said, with ill-concealed relief, "So, the disciplinary committee meets when?"

"This week," I said, a little stung. "Thursday."

"Okay," he said. "And what do you think will happen?"

It was surreal to discuss these things with him, he who was, by every measure save a genetic one, a stranger. I found myself affronted by his blunt questioning. It was remarkably easy to dislike your own parent, I thought, as I watched him staring at me with a comically serious expression on his face; it was just as easy as it was with other people.

"Well," I said. "It seems likely that they will vote to expel me."

And that was true. The committee—made up of three students and three faculty—would have no choice, really. It was not really, I am sad to say, an ambiguous case.

"Okay," said my father again, nodding. Americans, I thought unkindly, always *okay*. "What then?"

"I'm sorry?"

"What will you do," said my father, "after that?"

I nodded to show I'd understood the question, then, showily, so he could not mistake it, let my eyes roam lazily about the room, as if I were only just considering all the things I might do. You couldn't just bludgeon someone into intimacy, I thought peevishly; we hadn't even ordered yet.

"I haven't really thought about it, to tell you the truth."

I saw it hit the mark. My father's mouth twitched slightly at the corner—and I had a little flare of memory, then, of having seen that twitch before, many years ago, as a child.

But I was not telling the truth. I had thought about what would happen next, of course, like anyone whose life is about to change completely. The truth was that I had an attachment in that dreary town. It was, I would be the first to admit, not without its flaws: it was furtive, it was marred by the presence of my love-object's spouse, but in spite of its shortcomings, it had given me no small happiness. There was no universe in which I could communicate any of this to my father, but there it was nevertheless. When I thought of life after the demise of my medical career, it was of this connection that I thought.

"Let me ask you this," said my father. By now he had recovered himself. He was determined to be patient at all costs. He said, clearly and slowly, "Do you want to practice medicine?"

I pretended to give this serious question some serious thought. "No," I said. "Not particularly."

I hoped, childishly, that this would hurt him, but he seemed not to care, and then he gave me a look I couldn't quite read, a long, evaluative look.

We must have ordered at some point, because the tea had come: two pots, one for each of us, each in its quilted, patterned cozy, and a plate of toasted, buttered crumpets, which my father eyed suspiciously. With the air of someone who has waited far too long for something, he poured his tea into his cup, eschewing the strainer and adding too much milk, so that the liquid in his cup was practically white, with dark, unappetizing bits of tea leaf floating at the top. He took a sip, a look of distaste crossing his face, and then carefully replaced his cup on his saucer. It was remarkable, really, how wrong that had gone, and for a moment I forgot what we had been talking about.

"Excuse me," he said, calling over the waitress. "Could I have a glass of iced water?"

I wished he would not address her quite so loudly, and felt a fleeting alliance with her, against him, and hoped she would not notice his untouched tea.

Then he turned his attention back to me. It was clear now that he had made a decision and was about to inform me of it.

"If I were you," he said, "I'd withdraw. Before the committee meets. In fact, I'd do it today."

"It's Saturday," I said.

He made a gesture of impatience, but he had his own agenda now, and that trumped the irrelevance of what I'd said.

"On Monday, then."

"Monday," I repeated, nodding. How useless, I thought. All this, so far, was meaningless. But then he said something I did not expect.

"I'm going to have them make you an offer. I mean, at the med school. You can withdraw from here." He gestured vaguely out the window at, I presumed, the city of Ottawa. "You can take some time, let's say two, three months, just to clear your head, and we'll get something together for you."

I lowered my cup of tea slowly back to the safety of its saucer. "Something together?" I said, and he raised his palm.

"Just something administrative, you know, nothing glamorous, while you figure things out, but it'll carry you through."

"I—" I tried again. "In California?"

He gave me a strange look.

"Yes, of course," he said. "In California."

He seemed to think of something else then—like he was poised on the brink of it, unsure. Then he decided: yes, he would proceed.

"I haven't . . ." he began, and I saw that he was no longer at ease; his eyes flicked across the tablecloth, avoiding mine.

"Always been the best at . . . keeping in touch," he said, finally. He shook his head, as though he were disagreeing with himself. "But the past is in the past."

And now there was a little silence, a pause, in which he

could not even bring himself to look at me, to see how I'd received this. Of course, I thought, I understood the transaction now: job offer as apology for a lifetime of neglect. It was clear to me, and yet I was not made of stone; I could not help but thaw to him a little.

"That's very generous of you," I said. "The offer, I mean."

He shrugged. The waitress had brought over his ice water by now, and gingerly, as if one could not be sure even of such a familiar beverage in an establishment like this, he took a sip.

"Think it over, if you want," he said.

I nodded. I had a brief, hideous vision of myself in a convertible, driving down a sunny avenue lined with palms. The conversation with my father and its unexpected offer of employment had cast my present situation in a different light. It *was* probably foolish to think that a provincial, gray, rain-soaked place could keep me happy for a lifetime. And it was true that the love affair had given me pleasure, but a little voice, one I'd done my very best to ignore, told me I would never have it quite the way I wanted. After all, I thought, I was only twenty-three. Was there not, I thought, some other, better love around the corner?

By the time this long and strange remembrance of my father was over, my spaghetti had grown cold. I had to start the microwave again. When it was done, I sat down at the plastic table and ate—the noodles now unpleasantly rubbery—in silence.

18 It was just like me, I thought, back at my desk again, to dwell on the past. I had not thought of that visit of my father's in a long time, perhaps not in years, and I had been taken aback by just how vivid it had been. Still, there was nothing to be gained from going over matters like that again and again, like a dog with a bone.

Out of habit, I shuffled a pile of papers on my desk, recapped a pen, and straightened a few things. It was just, I thought with a heavy heart, the kind of thing a glorified secretary would do. What a strange way to pass the day: to encounter a stranger in the break room, then to overhear by chance an unflattering remark about yourself, and then, somehow as a consequence, to be lost in a long, detailed, and remarkably realistic daydream about a visit your father paid you more than twenty years ago! It was no wonder I— But that was when I saw that, amid my flurry of tidying and rearranging, I had taken the folded piece of stationery out of my pocket and spread it flat against my desk with the palm of my hand. Not the one I'd found in the pocket of my father's coat, but the one the guest lecturer had given me in the Arboretum, the one with the name Daniel Shriver written on it, in clearly legible script, as if whoever had written it could not afford to be misunderstood. I spread it flat again; I smoothed it a second time with my palm, more slowly, like I was stroking a cat. But, I thought, what are you thinking of doing here? With my index finger I traced the two convergent lines of the cross and the steeple.

Then another thought bubbled up: Wasn't that quite enough second-guessing? If the day's dillydallying had taught me anything, it was that now was a time for action. Indolence is the forerunner of death, I thought. I had read that somewhere, I was sure. I took a deep breath, picked up the telephone, and dialed the number for the Old Mission Hotel.

Perhaps this time—I thought—and then there was a click, and a slight pause, and then a cool, impersonal voice said, "Hello? Mr. Shriver? We've been expecting your call."

"Hello? Are you there?"

I cleared my throat. With considerable effort I produced a hoarse, "Yes."

"We've been trying to reach you," said the voice, and of course I recognized it immediately, it was the smooth-faced young man from the reception desk, the one who'd told me my watch had stopped.

"I see," I said. Somehow, events were moving out of my control, and I had a perverse desire to simply hang up the phone and walk out of my office, to never hear the name Daniel Shriver again.

"About your bag," said the young man.

"About my bag," I parroted. "Yes."

"It seems you left it behind during your stay."

"Yes," I said again.

"Should I send it to the address on file?"

I felt like a man swimming deep in the ocean, trying to read a sign being held above the surface. The man was clearly speaking to me, but nothing he was saying was making any sense. The address on file. The image of the open house sign, sitting like a white bird on the lawn, flitted through my mind's eye. Laboriously, I thought it through. Nothing would be gained by having the bag sent there.

"No, thank you," I said, finding my voice at last. "I can come pick it up myself."

"That is excellent news," said the young man, and his tone suggested he really was pleased by it. "When can we expect you?"

I eyed the little clock on my shelf—it was now ten minutes to one. I could be there in twenty-five minutes, if I didn't dawdle. I was just about to propose this time to the voice on the telephone when it occurred to me that perhaps there was something undignified about dropping everything and rushing over right away. The Swedish policeman, for example, would not have done so; I was sure of it. If he was no Stepin Fetchit, then neither would I be.

"Five," I said, "around then."

"Excellent," said the voice on the other end. "We'll have it waiting for you."

After what seemed like an eternity of waiting it was a quarter to five, and I gathered up my things and prepared to leave. All afternoon my thoughts had been circling around the phone call and the mysterious piece of luggage I was about to claim, circling and circling like water circles a drain. As I passed the mailboxes in the hallway I stuck my hand out and patted the inside of mine. The gesture was pure habit, and I'd already gotten the mail that day, so I was startled when my fingers brushed up against something. I stopped. What was it?

It was a single sheet of paper, a flyer advertising an up-coming lecture. I would not have given it a second thought were it not for the bizarre title, which read, in block letters, AMERICAN HOLOCAUST. The speaker was being hosted by the history department, read the information below, as part of an ongoing lecture series, and here was a grainy photo of the speaker himself, a strong-featured older man with white hair, wearing a dark V-neck sweater. For a moment I had a flicker of recognition—I've seen this man before! But the feeling just as quickly dissipated. Not *everything* is connected, I thought, weary of myself. He was merely like countless academics before him: pale and besweatered. His name looked vaguely French.

Well, that was just ridiculous, I thought, crumpling the flyer up into a ball and dropping it in the wastepaper basket. This was a university, not a tabloid newspaper. *American Holocaust* indeed, I thought, shaking my head; everyone knew that such a thing did not exist.

19 I drove west through campus, and when I reached the oleander-lined driveway of the Old Mission Hotel, the foothills in the distance were just beginning to purple, and I could see above the hedge that the late-afternoon sun had steeped the red-tiled roof in a burnished coppery color. It really was a lovely building, I thought, with its gently sloping lines and thick white walls, to which the fading light had lent a rosy glow. Its loveliness has stayed with me. I can't seem to cancel my intention of going back to visit it, though of course there are many reasons that is no longer possible; I am told that not a brick remains.

It took my eyes a moment to adjust to the gloom of the lobby. Here, I saw, day or night had no meaning, the same bluish light suffused the windowless space at all hours, and the same faint music pulsed from the omnipresent sound system. My *own* pulse gave a little shudder and skip forward when I caught sight of the smooth-faced young man behind the reception desk—but, I thought, get ahold of yourself. Of course the young man is here, you only just spoke with him on the phone. If you're going to have a small heart attack each time you encounter an employee of the hotel, how exactly do you plan to solve a murder?

He was in the middle of helping a professional-looking young woman with dark hair and a suitcase beside her; they were conferring in low tones, and if he'd noticed my arrival at all, he gave no sign. Someone had added a vase of white lilies to the front desk, their stamens slick with yellow pollen, and though I was standing several yards away, I could smell their funereal scent distinctly. To my right I could see that the dark wooden bar was open for business, the row of red votive candles had been lit, and a few patrons with drinks were scattered along its length. I had the impression that the hotel was now more robust, somehow, more lively, than it had been the first night, when I'd crossed the lobby with the intoxicated guest lecturer, as if that had only been a dress rehearsal, and this was the real thing. But this, I reflected, was mere silly imagining; of course it had been a hotel, and to the same degree, all along.

The woman in front of me concluded her business with the front desk, snapped the handle of her suitcase smartly, and rolled it away, its wheels squeaking on the spotless floor, and suddenly the reality of my project came fully to bear. When I approached the desk I would be masquerading as Daniel Shriver, whoever that was, who had come to retrieve a bag he'd left behind. Really it should not fill me with dread the way it did. People did it all the time. The Swedish policeman— But before I could think what exactly the Swedish policeman would have done, I saw that the smooth-faced young man had finally noticed me. Looking up from his desk, he beckoned me forward with a small smile.

"How can I help you?"

"Hello," I said, stiffer than I would have liked. "I left a bag behind. Here," I added unhelpfully.

"Oh yes," said the man. "What was the name?"

I was suddenly overcome with embarrassment; I felt like an actor in a bad play. "Daniel Shriver," I said begrudgingly.

The young man nodded at the mention of "my" name and gave every indication that he was about to set some bag-retrieval process in motion, until he stopped completely, his attention suddenly arrested by something else. Following his line of sight, I saw that it was the bouquet of white lilies I had noticed before on the counter; they had wept a light, powdery dusting of yellow pollen onto the black surface.

"Excuse me for a moment," said the young man. Without warning, he dipped behind the counter and surfaced hold-ing a small cloth, which he used to wipe away the offending pollen—a fastidious gesture, like a woman wiping away a bit of makeup. I watched, transfixed.

"Sorry about that," said the smooth-faced young man. He gave me his little smile again. It was warm but impersonal, like the smile of a young Buddha.

"Yes, your bag, Mr. Shriver," he went on. "How could I forget? We spoke on the phone earlier, if I'm not mistaken."

I nodded, my mouth suddenly dry again. Did he recog-nize me, I wondered, from the night we'd crossed paths in the lobby and he'd told me my watch had stopped? Would he put two and two together—and suspect? But it occurred to me, of course—I could have been "Daniel Shriver" then, too.

"Yes," I said. "That's me."

The young man appeared to check something below my line of sight.

"Oh, that's right," he said brightly, looking up. "We did have your bag, but your representative has already picked it up for you."

"My—" I said. "I'm sorry. My what?"

"Yes," said the smooth-faced young man, as if this were all to be expected. He gave no sign that he noticed my agitation. "Don't worry, she hasn't gone far."

"She?" I managed to get out.

"Yes," said the young man, and he thought for a second, remembering. With a look and a slight tilt of the head, he indicated the other end of the lobby.

"She's at the bar."

How unpredictable life is, I thought. In the morning one is a glorified secretary, and at night one's "representative" has retrieved a bag one has attempted to pick up while masquerading as someone else.

I thanked the young man and made my way toward the bar. I was strangely calm, as if this were how I had imagined my evening unfolding all along. It was clear that the young man at the front desk found nothing odd in the arrangement. As I approached the bar, I scanned its patrons for anyone obviously attached to a piece of luggage, but I saw nothing more remarkable than a few women with handbags. I cast a glance back at the reception desk, but the young man was already helping a new set of guests, a harried-looking couple with a small, fidgety child. I turned my attention back to the bar. There was, I saw, one female figure who appeared to be unaccompanied, and the more I studied her the more I had a strong impression of familiarity, like the whiff of a familiar scent. I know the set of those shoulders, I thought; I know that brassy hair. I had approached this particular hair-and-shoulder combination not so long ago, from the very same angle, amid the blue skies and birdsong of the Arboretum. So this was my representative, I thought. It was the guest lecturer.

I stood somehow immobilized a yard or two behind her, like a butler waiting at table. Tonight she was wearing a suit very similar to the one she'd worn the night we'd met, except instead of lavender, this one was white. White jacket, white pants. Who was she, and why had she decided to attach herself to me? Not only to my waking life, but to my dreams. I looked around her for a bag of any kind but saw only on the bar in front of her a long red lacquered-looking pouch. Clearly a woman's, clearly not Daniel Shriver's, clearly not a suitcase. There was no bag, I realized. It was all a bizarre ploy to bring me face-to-face with the guest lecturer again.

Just then there was a loud crash from the front end of the lobby. The vase of white lilies had fallen to the floor in front of the reception desk and shattered. Water was dripping steadily from the counter's lip, and the mother was remonstrating with her little boy, her hand viselike on his arm.

When I turned back to the bar, the guest lecturer was gone.

In her place, balanced on the stool she had recently vacated, was an object I recognized, a slim leather briefcase, its gold buckles glowing faintly in the candlelight. I looked around me, to the dimly lit couches, but she was nowhere to be seen.

"Excuse me, did you see the woman who was sitting here?"

I had spoken to the bartender, who had materialized in

front of me, tall and unfriendly-looking, with a grid-like tat-
too peeking out from under each shirtsleeve. In answer to my
question, he gave me a quizzical look.

"Yes," he said. His voice was deep, and not a jot friendlier
than the look of its owner.

"Do you know if she's staying here at the hotel?" I asked,
attempting a breezy tone. I was met with silence, then an arch
look, and then the bartender began polishing a glass with a
white cloth napkin. It occurred to me suddenly that because
of the way my question was phrased, he might suspect me of
harboring romantic inclinations toward the guest lecturer,
and I hurried to acquit myself of this suspicion.

"It's just that I think she may have forgotten her bag," I
said, with a gratuitous gesture at the briefcase.

We studied the bag together. The implausibility of it was
immediately apparent. The briefcase, as I had remarked earlier on my first visit to the Old Mission Hotel, just did not go
with the woman.

"Or," I said, "it may be mine, come to think of it."

Now that I had embarked upon this grotesque conversation, I was having trouble drawing it to a close. The bartender
seemed not to have even a glimmer of interest in what I did
with the briefcase in front of me, and yet words continued to
pour out of me like water from a tap.

"The man at the front desk told me someone had picked
something up for me. I wonder if this could be it?"

Some time ago, over by the front desk, the little boy who'd
knocked over the flowers had begun to wail, his high voice
rising against the background of the ambient music like a
mourner's, and now he grew louder and more piercing, making

it difficult to think clearly. And yet, I thought, what is there to think? The bartender was still blank-eyed, polishing his glass. I made a pretense of looking the briefcase over, of lifting it by the handle and turning it from side to side, and then, feeling more and more like a third-rate understudy, I produced a little crowing noise of recognition.

"It *is* mine!" I said. I lifted it by the handle and brought it to rest at my side. It had a pleasing weight to it. The bartender continued to watch me with elaborate disinterest.

"I'll be on my way, then," I said, stepping back from the bar, briefcase in hand. "Thank you for your help."

It had been convenient, I reflected, as I crossed the lobby, for my own purposes, that the bartender was such a surly, silent type. And yet wasn't it surprising, I thought, that in an establishment so characterized by its professionalism, such a person had found employment? I skirted the front desk, where I saw that the shards of vase had been swept neatly into a dustpan and looked now as though they were patiently waiting for someone to take them away.

The briefcase was empty. I switched the light on in the car, incredulous, but it was as empty as if I'd just purchased it from a shop. And not just this, but the lining was pristine, soft and dry. It could not be the same briefcase, I thought, as the one I'd discovered on my first visit to the Old Mission Hotel, beneath the desk in the guest lecturer's hotel room, because not even the most virtuosic of dry cleaners could have removed that mysterious thick liquid from the delicate material without leaving a stain. (Of course, I told my former self irritably, that liquid could not have been blood—that had been very melo-dramatic of me.)

Two briefcases, I thought, switching off the light in the car. *Two identical briefcases.* It was undoubtedly all very strange. Why would the guest lecturer be so eager for me to have an empty briefcase? Why had she called herself my representative and waited for me at the hotel bar, but then disappeared before we'd had a chance to exchange even a single word? And of all the things one could leave at a hotel, a briefcase seemed to fall into the category of vital things, things one would be unlikely to forget.

I shut the briefcase, closed the buckles, and laid it gently on its side in the passenger seat, as if I were putting it to bed. I had in mind a moment of relaxation; I let a breath escape me. It had been a very long day—it was hard to believe that only that morning I'd been interrupted by Alex Foss in the break room. It seemed much longer ago.

I looked out at the sky, where dusk was edging into night. And that was when I saw that something was stuck under my windshield wiper, obscuring the view. I'd been in such a hurry to open the briefcase that I hadn't noticed.

Suddenly I was alert again, as if I'd been pricked with a pin. What was the matter with this hotel and pieces of paper on windshields? I felt an indignation rising in me, pure and white; I hailed it like an old friend. If I had not already spent enough time in that soulless lobby, I would have gone back inside to complain. Surely a person should be able to park his car somewhere for ten minutes without it being blanketed by nonsensical papers, to who knows what end? I looked around, and sure enough, each windshield in the lot had its own little sheet. Like the last, this one had the look of something badly photocopied, but unlike its predecessor it had no image, only text. *THE MISSIONS*, it read, in angry black lettering, *WERE FURNACES OF DEATH*.

20

I crossed the reservoir under a black night sky; I rolled my window down, took a breath, and felt the sting of the cold air at the bottom of it. I just needed a little time to think, I told myself, that was all. The smell of the sea was very far inland tonight, I thought, and took another, more modest breath through my nose. So many things had happened, developments of all different weights and categories; it would take time and some distance to put everything in order. Now I came up out of the reservoir and onto the ridge, where a white sickle moon was visible intermittently through the tops of the pines. Triage, I thought, smiling a little to myself at the word, because if the day's events had taught me anything it was that I was *not* a doctor.

I set the briefcase down in the foyer, where it looked unconvincing, like a prop for a play. The clock above the stove read five minutes to eight. On the drive home I'd imagined myself sitting at the table with a paper and pen and writing down all that had occurred while it was still fresh, but now, in the tinny light of the kitchen, with the monolithic black pressing in against the windows, this plan looked overly ambitious. It had all been so exhausting—it would probably be best to direct my remaining energy toward tasks I knew I could accomplish, like making a sandwich and going to bed. Yes, I thought, a quiet sigh escaping me, that would likely be best. I opened the refrigerator door and, ignoring the pot of spaghetti that sat reproachfully on the top shelf, I took out the jar of mayonnaise, a can of salmon, and two slices of bread. I ate my sandwich standing over the kitchen sink; then I washed the knife and cutting board and went to bed.

I'd been looking forward to reading my book—to escaping for a while into someone else's concerns. But after several minutes, I was forced to return to the beginning of the chapter and start it again. I read more slowly this time, concentrating on putting the words together carefully, and yet the sentences refused to reveal any of their meaning to me, and I found myself going over the same lines again and again, puzzling at certain banal phrases, at descriptions of the scenery and the weather. In the end I gave up, put the book down, switched off the light, and went to bed mildly dissatisfied. I still could make neither head nor tail of the plot; the only thing I'd gleaned from my efforts was that the police inquiry had moved, for a reason unintelligible to me, to a group of tiny islands north of the Arctic Circle. These islands were apparently of great personal interest to the author—he had included several pages' worth of description of their unique landscape, industry, and inhabitants. Early in the book, I suppose, such material could have been a welcome addition to the "atmosphere," but so late in the investigation, frankly, it was difficult to see the point.

The next morning when I arrived at the university I found myself heading in the direction not of my own building but of the medical school library, a modest building adjacent to the hospital. The attendant behind the desk at the entrance was always the same—a kindly bald man who every Monday set out cookies and a samovar of tea. I nodded to him as I descended to the basement level, where I knew there was, next to the periodicals, a gigantic globe—almost as tall as I was, illuminated from within by a mysterious light source, and set at an angle on its spindle. I gave it one gratuitous spin and watched the patchwork countries flow beneath my fingertips, and then brought it to rest. Here was Germany: a small, cracker-shaped country wedged between Poland and France. Here in little tiny writing was Hamburg, Munich, Frankfurt, and Berlin . . . But Tübingen was nowhere to be seen. All I had wanted was the basic information—was it in the south? The north? And yet, I thought, deflated, what would the point of that be, exactly? Even if I did happen to encounter Mr. Reinecke again, I could not pretend to have just remembered something about Tübingen. How exactly, I thought, giving the globe a final and unfriendly push, did I imagine I would work that into the conversation? *Oh, Mr. Reinecke, how funny to run into you here—I have just remembered that Tübingen is in the south.*

When I opened the door to my office, I saw that the small red eye on my telephone was blinking.

Someone has already called this morning, I thought, which would be unusual, or alternatively they had called in the night after I'd gone, which would be stranger still. I stood in the center of my office, considering. Push the button and get it over with? Or delay? There was something ominous about that light and its blinking. That, and it was too early to listen to the voice of another human, someone I knew, speaking my name with some demand—the thought was repulsive.

I would go and make a pot of coffee first, I decided, before I let whatever was behind that red eye intrude. A pot of coffee and a good, careful thinking over of all of yesterday—then I would feel more equipped to push the button marked play. I set the leather briefcase down gently on the floor beside the desk.

The hallway was deserted; the break room, too. Someone had ripped open a packet of sugar and spilled it in an impressive arc across the counter; I tidied it up, rinsed out the coffeepot, and set it to brew.

Now, I thought, I will open my mind to the investigation; I will welcome in whatever thoughts that come. It was clear that the most important sequence of events had begun with the young man at the front desk's unexpected announcement that my bag, or rather, Daniel Shriver's bag, had been picked up by a "representative," and culminated in the vase of white lilies falling to the floor with a crash. With the briefcase, I corrected myself, with its appearance, and then, I thought, or was the last in the important sequence of events in fact the piece of paper wedged under my windshield wiper? *The missions were furnaces of death*, it read, a phrase not easy to forget. But in the end, after some thought, I rejected the connection. It was bizarre and irritating, whoever was doing it should be reprimanded, and not only that, but the logistics of it were difficult to understand, but it had nothing to do with me, and I would not waste my time thinking of it.

Next I had a moment of doubt. Because I hadn't actually seen her face—had it really been the guest lecturer sitting there at the bar with her back to me? I closed my eyes and pictured her: that brassy hair in the reddish candlelight, the white of the suit jacket. It had to be her.

On the counter, the coffee was brewing; it was sputtering loudly and with abandon. As much as I would have liked to make some headway with regards to the investigation, over and over again I found myself at a standstill. There were the components: the vase of lilies, the brassy hair against the suit jacket, the briefcase on the stool. But, while I could catalogue them, I had greater difficulty fitting them into any larger scheme. Why did I need an empty leather briefcase? Why hadn't the guest lecturer stayed to chat? These did not appear to be questions that could be answered merely by spending more time thinking about them.

Without warning the figure of Mr. Reinecke came to mind, unbidden, with his head of blond hair and graceful way of moving about the room. I could picture him now, over by the refrigerator, mug of coffee in hand, his eyebrows raised interrogatively.

Just then the coffee maker clicked itself off with an air of quiet triumph.

Tübingen, Tübingen, I whispered softly to myself. *Yes, I imagined myself saying. Lovely place, I visited there in the spring of '85.* I felt a sudden pang of loss, as if an opportunity that had been promised to me had just been taken away.

———

I let myself into my office and raised the blinds, admitting a bleary half-light that bathed the contents of the room in a new kind of dinginess. I had entered the room with every intention of listening to the message on my answering machine, but now I no longer felt capable of such a task. Instead I propped a thick white piece of mail against the telephone so that it obscured the blinking red light. Then I sat for a while, without moving. I had the semiconscious feeling that I was falling prey to the same kind of interlude as I'd experienced yesterday in the break room, another precise little daydream, and from the same period of my life—those days in Ottawa leading up to my withdrawal from medical school.

We'd had an argument in the night, and when I rolled over and reached out in the morning upon waking, I had the disconcerting experience of grasping at empty space: a rumpled sheet and a deserted pillow. We *had* argued, but still, I thought, as I swung myself around and out of bed, leaving before dawn was a little extreme. I thought I had made it clear that the morning ahead was an important one, and I would have liked some company at breakfast. Still, I was prepared to forgive it. In those days I was in the habit of forgiving a lot.

It was not until I had made myself a cup of coffee and sat down at the tiny table in the kitchen that I noticed the note sitting in front of me.

N, it began.

*Can't go on much longer like this. Part of the trouble is me,
of course, and my "situation" as always. But now it's—
[this was crossed out and abandoned] Why won't you be
honest with me about what happened last week? I can't
believe, as it seems you would like me to, that it was all just
a "misunderstanding." That didn't seem to be the way the
doctors were treating it anyway. If you could have them call
me from the hospital, why not just tell me the truth? And—
another thing—didn't want to mention it at the time, but
for me to be your emergency contact! Darling, it isn't wise.
It was only by chance that I was alone and could come
straightaway. Especially if you [crossed out] if it should
happen again, [here the word "which" had been vigorously
crossed out] and it is my [an unintelligible word] that it
might. In any case, I can't help you very much if you won't
tell me the truth about it. I'm sorry but I think it's in my
own best interest to keep my distance until you can speak
honestly with me about this.*

Your F

It was written on a page torn from a book of notepaper I'd
bought from a shop on Lady Ellen Place that sold imported
British stationery (F, the only child of wealthy, doting parents,
had a blithe disregard for other people's possessions) and was
accompanied by a sad little key—the spare key, I realized, F's
key, looking quite unequal to the drama of the situation.

I opened the drawer of the desk by the door and put the
note and the key inside. I would give all that some thought
later, I decided. I checked the clock on the desk and saw that

if I didn't leave right away, I would be late. But as much as I wanted to, I couldn't quite impress the spirit of haste upon my limbs, and slowly, like a sleepwalker, I sat down at the chair at my desk to put on my shoes—first one, then the other. I rose, took my coat from its hook by the door, wound on a thick wool scarf, and ducked out into the rain to meet my father.

When I surfaced from my daydream the light in the room had taken on an unpleasant, congealed quality, and I was left with a pit of resentment. It was just like me, I thought bitterly, to dwell on the past—the past, the past, always the past. How did people do it? I wondered. How did they insert themselves into the present?

21

There was still so much leftover spaghetti, I thought with a heavy heart as I drove home, and still I found myself turning down the road where the dingy little Chinese place was, in the crook of the valley, where I gave my order to the unsmiling woman in a hairnet at her window. We should have been on a first-name basis by now, I thought, as I sat to wait, trying to warm my hands on a cup of watery tea. I'd been her regular customer for at least twenty years, but instead things seemed to be progressing in the opposite direction: if she had once been merely indifferent, now she was unmistakably hostile.

At home, I opened the waxed paper boxes: green beans swimming in red oil, noodles in a brown sauce, a pea-flecked, perfectly level block of fried rice. I ate too quickly, and then felt thirsty, a little sickly, and in an unpleasant mood. I could not be expected to think of my father now, I told myself, for god's sake a man must have a break. Also, I thought, it was time to stop pretending I might eat the rest of the spaghetti. I hoisted the pot above the sink and watched as the noodles clumped sluggishly down the drain. I should not have made so much, I thought, as I ran the hot water and the garbage disposal. I filled a tall glass with cloudy water from the tap and took it to the bedroom, where I brushed my teeth, changed my clothes, installed myself under the covers, and opened my book.

The detective and his colleagues had left the Arctic islands, so that was a relief. Now there were some pages devoted to another questionable subplot—the one about the detective's friend, who owned the boarding facility for racehorses. He and the detective had been great friends in their youth and now the detective was eager to reconnect, although the friend, so far, appeared significantly less interested. The only eyewitness to the murder, incidentally, had been the victim's horse. As far as the investigation went, it was just as irrelevant as the islands interlude, but for some reason I minded it less. My intention had been to read until I felt sleepy and then turn out the light, but instead I found that the more I read, the more awake I began to feel, and alongside it a growing sense that the key to the whole book, the beginning of the end of the investigation, as it were, was close at hand. When the part about the racehorse-keeping friend drew to a close, the book entered a moody, somewhat aimless passage that seemed to me to be signaling clearly what it was, that sequence so familiar to all readers of the genre: the little lull in the action before the killer is revealed.

All the telltale signs were there: the detective had been transferred off the case; the detective had been spending a lot of time just as various professionals had instructed him not to, i.e., drinking, smoking, and brooding alone. The police chief had ordered that the case be put on the back burner, for lack of any new developments. Deep winter had turned into an anemic spring, and the detective felt obliged to call on a colleague of his who had been diagnosed with cancer. I had— any reader would have—every reason to believe that sooner or later the bulk of the evidence would begin to tip in the direction of one of the suspects: Would it be the neighbor? The estranged son? The serial killer known to have once operated in the region? A pleasant sense of anticipation washed over me, and I put the book down for a moment, splayed open on the coverlet to keep my place. I listened absentmindedly to the mannered two-note shriek of the crickets outside. Through the crack in the window I could feel the sharp edge of cold night air; I could smell the damp salt breath of the sea, but there I was, warm beneath the blankets, and, for this moment at least, content. If only real life could be like this, I thought, thinking of the book, its trends so clearly recognizable.

After these few moments of contemplation, I picked up the book again. When the character was first introduced, I felt only impatience. I could not understand what a vagrant former soldier had to do with anything, and I dismissed him as another one of the author's attempts at "atmosphere." And yet, several pages later, this vagrant had been fingered for the crime. Surely a red herring, I thought. An eleventh-hour distraction. But then a full-scale manhunt for the vagrant was underway. Still, I thought, it couldn't possibly be. It was unacceptable; you could not introduce the murderer some forty-odd pages from the end. I held out hope until it was clear that there would be no alternative: the vagrant ex-soldier and the murderer were one and the same. He had been in need of money, of course, and suffered from "psychological disturbances" from the war. Passing at random through town, he had had the good fortune to discover, also by chance, that the victim was despite appearances quite a wealthy woman, and so had called later that night to murder her on the floor of her barn.

I turned to the back of the book to have a look at the author photo—a smug man with a prominent jaw and a dark sweater stood, arms folded, against a backdrop of suitably Scandinavian snow. Well, I thought, addressing the photo, what a complete waste of time this has been. I do not appreciate this at all. Technically, there were a few chapters remaining, but I, for one, would not be reading them. Instead I tossed the book to the floor beside the bed, turned out the light, and fell headlong into what would prove to be another strangely relevant dream.

22 In my dream I was walking across campus on a brisk morning, the sun behind a cloud cover. This is pleasant, I thought to myself, and I put my hand in my pocket and began to whistle. I seemed to be heading in the direction of the Oval, though I had a difficult time judging how far away that was. The trees and sidewalk, although familiar, were devoid of any distinguishing characteristics. I had put my left hand in my pocket, because with my right hand I was carrying the briefcase. It seemed to have grown much heavier overnight. There was something in it, definitely; I could hear it knocking around, and it seemed as though what was inside was a heavy but not particularly large object, as if I were carrying an ingot of gold, or a candy bar made of lead.

In my dream, I was unperturbed by this. A thought arose: Might it be possible to look inside and see what the object was? But the dream version of myself did not seem interested in this question, and only kept on walking, whistling an unidentifiable tune. What a pleasure it was to walk alone, on campus, early in the morning, the dream-me thought. Why didn't I do it more often?

"Excuse me," said a deep and familiar voice. I turned in its direction. Sitting on a bench, amid a profusion of shrubbery, was Gerry Van Gelder, looking large and uncomfortable. When he spoke, he seemed ill at ease.

"Excuse me," he said again. "Do you know what time it is?"

"Of course," I said. Although I could not, in truth, say that I was happy to see him (he would delay me somehow, I felt, though from what I could not have said), I could certainly do him this service; I was brimming with goodwill. I transferred the briefcase to my left hand, and rolled back my shirtsleeve.

But when I looked down at my watch's face, I saw to my surprise that it was completely blank. Not only were there no hands, there were also no numbers. I gave it a little shake.

"I'm sorry," I said. "It looks like my watch has stopped."

I pointed the watch face in Gerry's general direction, though there was no way he could have seen it from where he sat. As it was, he barely glanced at it.

"That's too bad," he said, a strange, false note in his voice. "Don't you think you'd better stop, then?"

I stared at him. He really looked enormous sitting there on that little bench, among the overgrowth of vines. There was star jasmine all around him, and behind him a grassy lawn. Droplets of sweat were beading on his pasty, freckled temples.

"I don't think it will be a problem," I said coldly. I switched the briefcase into my other hand and kept walking; I didn't give Gerry another glance.

Time seemed to speed up in my dream, so that I encountered the second set of people very soon after I left Gerry, though they appeared to be in a completely separate location, standing on a sandy stretch of ground: a man, a woman, and a small boy, grouped together as if posing for a family portrait.

"Wait," said the little boy, and I stopped. I did not really feel like stopping, but I thought it would be impolite to simply ignore them. When I looked more closely at the little family arranged before me, it was apparent that they were from a different time. The man wore a dark old-fashioned suit with a waistcoat and a gold watch chain braced across his torso; the woman, who was considerably younger, wore a high-necked, somber-colored dress. The boy was in an elaborate white blouse, short pants, and black boots. He was not well, I saw at once. His eyes were shiny and feverish, each of his cheeks marked by a too-vivid pinprick of red.

"Won't you stay with us?" said the little boy, and then he was wracked by a fit of coughing. His mother held a white handkerchief to his lips that, with his next cough, was immediately stained with blood.

"Our son," she said, lowering her voice. "Our son has typhoid. We leave for Florence tonight. We think the doctors will be better in Italy. We've chartered a boat, and we think it would be best if you came with us."

"I'm sorry," I said. "That's very kind, but I'm in the middle of something."

She looked pained at my reply and cast a questioning look at her husband, who remained stony-faced.

"What you are planning to do," she said. "Please reconsider. We know that place."

Here she looked at her husband again. "Don't we know that place?"

He nodded, but just barely; he seemed determined to stay out of it.

"It's . . ." she said. "There has already been so much death there—" Here she was interrupted by her child, who, gripping at her skirts until she bent down to attend to him, began to whisper something furiously in her ear.

"Hush," said his mother. A new fit of coughing from the little boy distracted them both, and I took the opportunity to withdraw from view.

The dream scene was closing in on me now; I had the sense that I would have to pick up the pace considerably if I wanted to reach my destination in time, but I found myself veering off the sidewalk I'd been walking on, drawn by some current into a thick and wooded area. The ground was covered in a layer of old strips of eucalyptus bark that crunched underfoot.

Now I entered a clearing in the trees, where a young man with sunlit golden hair was reclining in a leisurely attitude on top of a large raised rectangular object that I recognized, after a moment's reflection, as a tomb. Then I saw that the young man was, in fact, Mr. Reinecke.

"Oh," I said, startled, "I wasn't expecting you." Self-consciously I ran a hand through my hair; I positioned the briefcase just out of his line of sight.

"No?" said the dream-Reinecke. "I was expecting you, though."

He spoke slowly, lazily, and with not a hint of interest in my arrival. He was dressed differently than he had been when we'd met in the break room, in a white knit sweater that emphasized the glacial blue of his eyes, which were ringed with thick blond lashes. Suddenly I felt very conscious of the sunlight dappling the scene; it had settled in a large, yolk-like arrangement on his thigh.

"Wouldn't you like to stay?" he said.

"I—I'm afraid I can't," I said nervously, fingering the handle of my briefcase. The dream-Reinecke did not seem troubled by this. He merely picked an invisible piece of lint off his sweater and stretched his long legs so that they draped across the tomb. Just when I thought he would not speak again, he said:

"Of course, it's a big decision, it's understandable that you wouldn't want to stop. It's true what the lady said, though; it isn't a nice place. A lot of precedent there for that kind of thing, unfortunately."

Before I could ask what he meant, he—along with the tomb, the sunlit glade—disappeared from view. Now I was kneeling in the undergrowth, looking out through an opening in the manzanita at a dirt path winding my way. In the distance came the sound of feet hitting the earth. Someone was coming down the path, I thought, not just coming—*running*. She would be here any second now, I thought.

I am lying in wait, I thought. I looked down and saw that I had opened the briefcase. Am I? I thought. Am I lying in wait?

23

I woke with an unsettled feeling. The leather briefcase sat innocuously on the chair in the corner, as banal and impenetrable as ever. What had been inside it, in the dream? But already the "plot"—Gerry Van Gelder, I thought, Mr. Reinecke!—was fading from memory.

Later that morning I was in the hallway outside my office when some movement outside the window caught my eye. It was a group of graduate students one level below me—walking along the parking lot heading toward the center of campus. One of them had apparently just said something very funny; the whole merry little band was convulsed with laughter. They would be heading to the coffee shop connected to the museum, I assumed, and I was grateful not to have encountered them in the hall on their way out, as they could be loud and boisterous when they traveled like that in packs.

In the break room I noticed that a copy of the weekly paper was lying on the small white plastic table in the corner—the same paper in which I'd read the notice for my father's open house, the same paper in which, in what felt like a lifetime ago, I'd inadvertently read my own horoscope. But this was a new edition, of course, this week's edition, and I slid it toward me and began to flip through its pages.

This time is different, I thought. This time there is no Kirstie to disturb me; I can do whatever I want—I can read whichever part of the paper pleases me. If it's the horoscope I want to read, I can read it. I found the page and watched as my index finger slid along the little pictures of animals until it came to rest on the silhouette of the goat, with its slender, curving horns. I could feel my pulse beating faintly in my fingertip.

Dear Capricorn, the text beside the goat read. *This new moon will be in graceful angle to your ruler, so it's safe to expect that a happy romantic surprise is due. With that in mind, circulate! Be open to meeting new people—and in the meantime, this would be a good week to focus on getting in peak physical shape: So go ahead and join that gym you've been curious about. Sign up for that fitness class you've been considering.*

The coffee maker clicked itself off just then, and I turned to look at it as though it had just spoken aloud.

What?

What meaningless garbage was this?

Was this the same weekly paper I'd read before? I turned back to the front page. It was.

Well, I thought, pushing the paper away from me. *Well.* Unable to complete the thought, I stood, retrieved a mug from the cabinet, and poured myself a cup of coffee.

There's no reason to be so derailed by this, I admonished myself. So you read a horoscope recently, a horoscope that led you to believe you were on the right track looking into your father's death. Today you have read a horoscope in the same paper with no bearing on anything, a horoscope filled with gibberish, nothing to do with you. So what? It changes nothing.

"Get ahold of yourself," I said quietly, and gripped the edge of the counter until I winced in pain.

Just so, I thought. The last thing you need is for someone to surprise you in the break room in a bizarre pose, muttering to yourself. I released my grip on the counter, wiped my forehead with a paper napkin, and went out into the hallway. I moved quickly, giving myself up to the thoughts that came.

Could it be? The idea growing in me now unchecked— could I have been wrong about everything? But, I protested, there had been that feeling, upon returning from my father's house, when I'd sat at my kitchen table to watch the fog roll in from the sea, the feeling that I'd set something in motion. That sense—I'd had it so clearly. Was it so extraordinary to think? But—I stopped short, and some coffee from my cup sloshed onto the ground. Could my recent activities truly be called "looking into my father's death"? What had I unearthed, exactly? I had read two horoscopes, one relevant, one not. I'd gone to a hotel, a restaurant, an open house; under a pseudonym, I'd acquired an empty leather briefcase. I'd declined to have intercourse with a mature and willing woman, and made myself god knew how many open-faced salmon sandwiches. Really, it could make a person weep.

When I reached the end of this last thought, I found myself at the door of my office. I eased it open, careful not to spill any more of my coffee, and sat down at my desk. There it was again, I thought with a shudder: in my excitement I had forgotten all about the red eye on the telephone—the envelope

I had propped against it yesterday had slipped, and the light was pulsing on and off patiently, biding its time like a watchful cat. Not now, I thought, replacing the envelope, not *this* distraction.

Maybe it would be nice to do something more tangible, I thought, to take a little break from musing on the two horoscopes, on the dreams, on how to position myself with respect to my father's death. Perhaps I should engage in some of my actual work, the activities I had recently heard so unceremoniously described by Alex Foss. But instead of settling down at my desk, it seemed that I was now pulling my chair over to the shelves on the wall, and reaching for a cloth-covered box I kept in the highest cubby. It had sat there, untouched, for years, and was covered in a layer of gray-brown dust, which now floated in unattractive clumps down to my desk. I sifted through some of the detritus of years past until I found one piece of paper, yellowing with age, folded in three.

Had a very bizarre phone call this morning. A man calling to say you'd drowned yourself in the Ottawa River. I don't know if he meant to gain entry with shock value, but he soon changed his story to say that you'd only tried to, and that you'd survived thanks to a curious passerby. He used all kinds of fancy psychological phrasing, but on the subject of how you two knew each other, exactly, he was quite vague.

On his name, too. "A friend," he said he was. Well.

As I have not had any news from the school I will assume you were unsuccessful in your attempt to end your life. It would be a very selfish thing to do, so I hope you got

*it out of your system. I gave him a good idea of how little
I would welcome another telephone call, and I must say
that if you find yourself tempted to give out my telephone
number to any other of your "friends," please reconsider.*

*In other news, we'd hoped to have puppies this spring,
but Jack did not take a liking to the neighbor down the
road's bitch as much as we'd thought. I can't say I blame
him. Write and tell me how you are.*

Mother

**24** An obscenely loud noise turned out to be the telephone on my desk.

"Hello?" I said.

"Hello," said a female voice. "This is Linda."

"Linda," I repeated, my mind a blank.

"In Professor Pindar's office," she said. "Are you free today? He'd like to see you."

I struggled to grasp these new and unwelcome concepts. What could I possibly say? "Today?"

"Yes, today," said Linda. "Would three work? That would be best for him."

A long pause followed.

"Three will work," I said finally.

"Perfect," she said. I could hear her fingernails clickety-clacking on the keyboard through the line. "I'm putting you down now."

I hung up the phone and held myself very still in the silence. Then I pushed a short burst of air out through my teeth. I no longer wanted to be in my office, I thought as I rose to my feet, at the mercy of whatever memorabilia and the telephone. If I wanted to be alone with my thoughts (and why Professor Pindar wanted to speak to me was one thought that, from the looks of things, circumstances behooved me to address), I would have to go elsewhere. That, and my coffee was now lukewarm. I would have to go and get another one, I thought, and then a movement outside my window caught my eye. It was a group of figures, heading back from the direction of the quad.

That group of graduate students, I thought, once again grateful not to have encountered them in the hallway.

But on second glance I saw that I was wrong. It was not, as I had previously imagined, a "group" of students, but two people walking side by side, and only one of them was a student. The second person was none other than the chair of my department, whom I was due to meet with at three: Professor Pindar. He was gesticulating wildly, his gray curls blowing in the wind. The other person—her substantial thighs clearly outlined in black running pants, her ponytail streaming behind her like a small, bright flag—was Kirstie.

**25** It was just like me, I thought, to think the worst of things, to go over every minor thing with a fine-toothed comb. There was no reason to think that whatever conversation Kirstie and Professor Pindar had been having outside was anything but benign. There was no reason at all to believe it had anything to do with me.

Linda was on the phone again at three, but she cupped one hand over the receiver and cast a glance at the closed office door, then she pantomimed knocking, and mouthed, contradictorily, *Go right in.*

Professor Pindar was bent over a stack of papers on his desk but motioned me into the room with one hand. He was more tired, less vital-looking than he'd appeared when I'd seen him through the window.

"Sit down," he said, indicating the chair across from him. "I'll just be a minute. You can move all that onto the floor."

I sat, noticing as I always did the room's most prominent decoration, which was displayed above the window in a long glass case: a broken wooden harpoon. Professor Pindar, it was said, was descended from New England whalers, though whether the fragment above the window had actually been wielded by his ancestors or was merely an evocative piece, I didn't know.

It occurred to me as I sat there waiting that it could be nice to make some remark about it—the harpoon, rather. I could not recall ever having mentioned it before, and I felt it might strike a friendly tone at the outset of our conversation. Who among us did not like to have their family heirlooms inquired about?

I thought then with some compunction of my mother's writing desk, which had been sitting neglected in my living room ever since her death. The truth was that I had never liked it, and I suspected that she hadn't liked it very much, either, because I could not remember ever having seen it in her house.

"Well," said Professor Pindar, with a final shuffling of the papers in front of him. "That should do it. Would you mind closing the door?"

When I returned to my seat it occurred to me that I still had yet to make a remark about the harpoon. Perhaps there was still time, I thought irritatedly to myself, but before I had a chance to think of anything, Professor Pindar said:

"Well. I don't want to presume anything, but I thought it might make sense for you and me to have a little chat."

He looked at me as though I might have some objection, and when I did not reply he went on.

"I just wondered if this hasn't been something of a difficult time for you."

A pause followed. I felt my face grow unpleasantly hot.

"I'm sorry," I said. "I'm not sure I understand."

"The things people say . . . Really, very few of them have

any idea what they're talking about," said Professor Pindar. "These decisions are much more complicated than you would think. Believe me, I've been on the committees."

Another bewildered silence. People were talking about . . . me? What could Kirstie have told him? Was it a crime to read one's horoscope in the break room? A crime to sit beside your colleague at a lunchtime concert? Or perhaps—was it possible that he had heard of my dinner with the guest lecturer?

"The impulse is to sensationalize, of course, but really, the time it takes for anyone to actually do anything; it's like watching ice melt."

"I see," I said. So, no, apparently, not about me. Or at least—I considered our conversation up until that point—so far it seemed to have been made up entirely of gibberish. And now too much time had passed for the remark about the harpoon. As usual, I had not moved quickly enough.

"Anyways," he said. "I just wanted to see how you were doing."

How I was doing? It occurred to me that because of his manner, and its place in the chronology of our conversation, he did not merely mean this as a casual, rhetorical question. And yet I could not imagine what, in particular, he could be referring to. Certainly it would be impossible for me to address how I really was: my investigation, my suspicions, my unease.

"Well," I said, a little stiffly, and then I made an expansive gesture that I hoped would suggest that my answer encompassed a whole variety of circumstances. "No complaints."

Professor Pindar looked as though he was waiting for me to say more.

When I didn't, he said, "I know that you and your father

weren't . . . Maybe you *were* close, I don't really know. But there was Barbara and the little girls, so that must have been . . ." He trailed off. "I can't imagine it was easy."

The nape of my neck pricked.

"And," he said, shifting uncomfortably, "I'm sure it can't help that that graduate student is in our department—in fact, I think you know each other—Kirstie Johanssen? She's the one who . . . knew your father, isn't she?"

He stopped now and began to rub his right eye with his index finger.

"I'm not going to pretend that this type of thing is my forte. All I'm trying to say is that from the outside, at least, the relationship looked a little strained. I mean, don't get me wrong, what an exceptional man and a great president for the university—but those kinds of people don't always make the easiest fathers, do they?"

A moment—a strained silence—passed. Then a strange set of conditions threatened to intrude. I held myself still, very still, because the image of Professor Pindar and Kirstie walking side by side was constantly on the edges, pressing in. I fixed my gaze on a point above Professor Pindar's gray head— incidentally, on the harpoon.

He turned, following the direction of my line of sight, and brightened visibly.

"Yes," he said. "Isn't that a hoot? As a matter of fact, my great-great-grandfather worked on the *Essex*. That's the whaler that inspired *Moby-Dick*."

Another little silence went by.

"Have you read it?" he asked.

I shook my head.

"No, well," he said. "It's very long. Took me several tries myself."

He turned away from me to look once more at the harpoon, and then turned back.

"These family things," he said. "They have a strange kind of power, don't they? Actually, I grew up in Nevada, about as far from the sea as the day is long, and never saw the ocean until I went to college, but that thing was my dad's, and when he died I thought I should give it a special spot."

Professor Pindar looked down at his hands and shifted a few times in his chair. It was evident that he was coming back now, back from this enjoyable discussion of the harpoon, to the topic at hand.

"Like I said," he began. "Not my strong suit, but I did want to let you know that even though your father has moved on, there's no need to worry at all about your position here. We value the work you do, and that's not going to change even though your father is no longer with us. Gosh"—here he laughed, a flurry of nervous, high-pitched sound—"that makes it sound like he died. All I mean is, since he's left the university."

The blinds were drawn, and a viscous yellow midafternoon sun was seeping in around the slats. It had turned out to be a clear day after all; it was always a clear day down here in the valley, and I had a momentary pang of longing for Ottawa and gray.

Strange, I thought. Ottawa again. I spent a few more moments there, in my memories, until I was interrupted by the sound of Professor Pindar clearing his throat. From the look on his face, it appeared that he had been trying to get my attention for some time.

"I don't want to take up too much of your afternoon," he said, not quite meeting my eye. "Did you . . ." he asked, and began again. "Was there anything you'd like to add?"

I considered. I looked past him and was once more struck by the thick yellow sunlight creeping in through the blinds.

"You might like to open your blinds."

"I . . ." said Professor Pindar. "I'm sorry?"

"May I?"

I crossed to the window and raised the blinds, and as if the physical activity had jogged my thoughts, I was finally able to think.

"What a nice view you have," I said. From his window you could see the red-tiled buildings in the western part of campus, and behind them, the gray-blue wash of the foothills, edging delicately into sky. "My window overlooks the parking lot."

"Well," said Professor Pindar. "I'm sorry about that, but when the new extension is finished there should be more room for everyone."

I held up a hand to cut him off.

"No need to apologize," I said. "It can be useful."

"I'm sorry?" he said again.

Now that the blinds were up, the sunlight was shining fully in Professor Pindar's face, and he was squinting into the glare.

"It can be a useful *view*," I said, clarifying, thinking of Kirstie in her running pants, her hand on Professor Pindar's arm.

Suddenly I felt my thoughts land, as a bird might land on a tiny perch.

"As a matter of fact," I began carefully, "there *is* something I want to add."

"Oh?" said Professor Pindar. But for all he had professed to want just this, he seemed less certain about it now.

"You say . . ." I said slowly. "You say you value the work I do here, and that I don't need to worry about my position."

Professor Pindar nodded, making one hand into a visor to shield his eyes. "Yes," he said, nodding vigorously. "Absolutely."

"But what . . ." I said, and I left the blinds then and crossed to the center of the room, "what exactly do I do here?"

"I'm sorry?"

"Would it not be accurate to describe my position as that of a 'glorified secretary'? And, more importantly, why do you pretend that my father has 'left the university'? Why is it so difficult for everyone to admit?"

"To admit what?"

But I found that despite it all, even I could not quite pronounce the words. "That there has been a death," I said, more quietly.

"I'm sorry," said Professor Pindar. "I didn't catch that. A death?"

Then I noticed something that had been staring me in the face all along, something I should have noticed a long time ago. It was a heavy black paperweight, crudely carved to resemble a whale, sitting on top of a stack of papers on Professor Pindar's desk.

Well, of course, I thought, of course he would have such a paperweight. How fitting, after all that talk of fathers, their possessions, and special spots. Was this, I thought, a chuckle rising in my throat, another heirloom?

"I know what you've been up to," I said softly.

"What?" said Professor Pindar.

"What?" I said. "I think you know each other, don't you, you and Kirstie Johanssen?"

"I'm sorry?"

"This morning," I said. "From my window."

My words seemed to be bubbling up all at once, and perhaps not in the right order; I took a breath in, to slow myself.

"This is a nice paperweight," I said, taking it in my hand.

"Thank you," said Professor Pindar. "I— Wouldn't you like to have a seat?"

What a stupid ornament, I thought. Here was a man not content to merely hang an ugly weapon in his office; he had also bought himself a paperweight, in case anyone was in danger of forgetting this fact, that he was descended from New England whalers. What a farce.

"My daughter gave it to me," he said, looking pained. He stretched out a hand as if to take it back, but I did not return it to him. It was heavy and smooth, a pleasure to hold in my hand. Not just a pleasure, I thought, drifting away from the room, from Professor Pindar, from the sunlight that now poured robustly into the room; a feeling more fundamental, as if something I'd lost without knowing it had finally been returned.

"I think there's been some kind of miscommunication, somewhere along the line. Is someone . . . dead? You seem— have you had a loss recently?" said Professor Pindar. I could barely see him in the glare of the sunlight, but I could not mistake his tone.

Had I had a loss recently? I had moved to the door as if to go, but now I found myself turning back to consider the question. I looked over, casually, at Professor Pindar, who seemed to have shrunk against the wall.

"Have I had a loss?" I said softly, not quite to myself, not quite to Professor Pindar, but somewhere in between. "Life is just one loss after another, is it not?"

I could not even begin to say, I thought, the kind of loss I've experienced, of everything moving forward as I stood still.

26

My face in the elevator's mirror wore a grim, persistent smile, as if ready for an unkind word. Rather than shift it, I looked away. We dropped from the second floor to the first, and then to the basement level: the doors opened, and I stepped out into the atrium, the square-shaped, open core of the building, where a strangled sunlight filtered down from five stories above.

I had no strong sense of what I'd meant to do there. Now I moved toward the sad coffee cart in the corner, with its depressed barista and depressing simulacra of patio furniture, but then changed course and turned away—but not quite soon enough to avoid making eye contact with a group of postdocs from my own department, who, I was horrified to see, were seated at one of the wrought-iron tables. There was a quick, painful moment of recognition, and then a much longer one of limbo, as I stood there, unable to proceed. At last one young man, a midwesterner whose name I had forgotten, raised his hand in a small, uncertain wave. Behind me I heard the soft *ding!* of a microwave. Startled, I waved back. Then, overcome with embarrassment, I hurried off down one of the low-ceilinged corridors that spread warren-like from the atrium's central court.

I let myself into the first empty room, a lecture hall in the old style, with steps sloping down to a small stage. I moved down a dark row and slid into a seat, closed my eyes and attempted to catch my breath, and heard only the agitated rushing of my own blood.

Is someone dead? Professor Pindar had said— But I tamped that down, and found my thoughts returning to the atrium, to the friendly young man who had waved. Matthew—that was his name.

How many such overtures had there been, over the years? It was true that, earlier on, I had mostly overlooked them. And more recently? I could think only of the dinner invitation with the guest lecturer, a much more complicated situation than it had initially seemed, not to mention one I had gravely misinterpreted.

I felt the erratic beating of my heart slow a little, and I drew in a gasping breath. And what would life be like if I were the sort of person who waved casually at colleagues, who dispensed greetings like the enthusiastic Matthew? Quite probably I would also be a person who could say, without missing a beat, *And where is Tübingen? I haven't heard of it. Is it in the south?*

Why not rest for a minute? I thought. I settled myself more comfortably in my seat. I could hear the geriatric ventilation system as it pushed feeble currents of air around the room, and the placid tick of the clock on the wall. A warm, drowsy feeling spread over me, and I had let my eyes close—just for a moment—when I became aware of another sound, someone speaking at a volume just lower than intelligible.

"Excuse me," the person said again, this time more loudly,

and I opened my eyes to see a woman of late middle age standing over me. She wore a black felt hat with a narrow brim and
clutched to her side a shabby and commodious handbag that
overflowed with papers.

"Yes?" I said, taken aback. I had not seen, or heard, her
come in.

"Someone sitting there?" she asked unpleasantly, jabbing a
long finger at the seat next to mine.

"No," I said. "No, of course not."

My response seemed not to please her at all. If anything,
she now looked more aggrieved.

"Then *may*-be," she hissed, "you'd be so kind as to move
your . . ."

She gestured to the seat beside me.

"Paperweight," I said, and then, more quietly: "Yes, of
course."

I endured her perfumed advances as she settled with unhappy
noises into the seat beside me. She managed to contain her
bulging handbag on the floor before her and then turned her
attention toward the front of the room, where I saw that, to
my astonishment, a man was now standing at the lectern. A
distinguished-looking, silver-haired man who looked familiar,
though I could not quite place him. And his arrival—how had
I missed it?—was not the only new development. With the exception of a few empty seats here and there, the room was
now full of people, apparently waiting for whatever would be
happening onstage to begin.

"Thank you all for coming," said the silver-haired man.

His voice was quiet but had an air of authority that was impossible to overlook.

"I'm sure I speak for us all when I say how grateful I am to Professor Nahimana for hosting us, here in the belly of the beast. I know we've all been waiting for this day for a very long time."

A little ripple of applause.

"It is an honor to follow such an important talk by Dr. Baker, whose new work on Haus Wachenfeld is, I think we can all agree, really very exciting. I wonder, Jim"—he appeared to address someone in the front row—"I could not help recalling a line that has always struck me as a lovely turn of phrase, despite the context."

He closed his eyes for a moment, remembering.

"'Along the road of the Teutonic knights of old, the Reich must again set itself, to obtain,'"—here he paused again—"'um mit dem deutschen Schwert, dem deutschen Pflug die Scholle'—by the German sword, sod for the German plow."

This little recitation, incomprehensible to me, was met with a murmur of appreciation from the audience. He paused to sip primly from a glass of water and, shading his eyes with his hands, looked to the back of the room and said, "First slide, please, Melissa."

The hum of a slide projector, a whir, and click.

"I'd like to begin," he said, as the image behind him—a map, I now saw—expanded and contracted and now came decisively into focus, "on the island of Hispaniola."

He went on, but his voice faded from me as I became increasingly aware of my neighbor, who, in doing something with her handbag, had caused a thick bundle of folded papers to fall from the arm of her chair into my lap.

"Oh, I'm sorry—" I whispered, and in the midst of returning it saw that it was not, as I had thought, some type of elderly person's brochure, but a stack of small and poorly copied little texts, bound together with a dirty rubber band.

A chill, premonitory shiver passed through me. What, I thought, was that?

"So, as you can see, as the Spanish began to build their empire in the New World," the man at the lectern was saying, "they looked to Rome's expansion to justify their own."

I had seen such sheets of paper before, I thought. *THE MISSIONS*—I could have sworn I'd seen those grainy black letters, before she'd snatched the bundle, clawlike, back.

"In a letter home from Hispaniola, Álvarez Chanca quoted Cato: 'Delenda est Carthago.' Carthage must be destroyed."

He turned to the map behind him now, as if to explain some of its various features, but I found it difficult to follow, and I heard my own racing thoughts instead.

On the windshield of my car, at the hotel. And this man! I thought, suddenly energized by these thoughts, these connections, I had seen him before, too—on the flyer I'd found in my mailbox, advertising the lecture called "American Holocaust." (And once before that, at my father's open house—but that I did not recall until much later.)

"In the North America of the 1700s, this preoccupation with space takes on something of a different flavor," he was saying now, and he, too, seemed suddenly invigorated. "What is necessary to remember is that for the Franciscans, once the soul was Christian, the physical form was more or less expendable."

Now the slide showed two men hanging from a makeshift gallows, their bare feet dangling above the ground.

Yes, I thought, that's right. The missions were furnaces of death—it was all part of the same demented thing. Now the man at the lectern spoke again.

"What a consolation, truly, to in death return to the bosom of God."

The words fell on an eerie silence. The constant smacking noises my neighbor had been making suddenly came to a stop. These people, I thought, they were behind it all. The silver-haired man was the leader of this sinister bunch, and these—I looked around me now at the rapt faces shining palely in the darkness—were his followers. This conclusion struck me with the force of truth.

But what was the point? To be sure, if the missions really *had* been furnaces of death, that was unfortunate, but what did it have to do with any of these people? No one in this room was in any way responsible for any death at a mission; they had not even existed in the same century. I shivered and thought: This kind of preoccupation is like a disease, it is the saboteur of healthy living, I must get away from here at once.

"Oh," said the silver-haired man, and it was as though the room's acoustics had undergone a shift. The light was falling on his face in an unusual way, and he spoke with a soft, peculiar coldness. "I take it you think your hands are clean?"

I shifted uncomfortably in my seat. I must have misheard, I thought.

"Melissa," he said. "Could we have a little light?"

I sat, frozen in place, as a spotlight swung from the back of the auditorium toward the front. It slowed as it came closer to the stage, then hovered in the first row, as if hesitating.

"I was under the impression," he continued, "that it was you who said that they are dying out in a quick and easy way, and are being supplanted by a superior race?"

It was difficult to dismiss the obviously irrational feeling that he seemed now to be speaking directly to me.

"And that the better classes have been overwhelmed by the unrestricted breeding of inferior racial stocks?"

No, I told myself, it is not possible, and yet I found myself thinking furiously: Me? Me? Of course not.

"Farther back," said another man's voice, from the audience. The spotlight stirred and began to swing slowly away from the stage.

I cleared my throat. To answer these accusations would be to dignify them, I told myself.

"And was it not you . . ." said the silver-haired man now, that soft, cold voice caressing, trying to sneak a way in. "Wasn't it you who said—referring to the children, of course—wasn't it you who said, *Nits make lice*?"

"No," I whispered. "I never said anything like that."

"The first step," said my neighbor, her face turning suddenly to mine, "is to admit your guilt."

I shook my head vigorously. I wanted to say, *You are all mistaken*, but the moisture had emptied from my mouth. The light had made its way to our row now, and I was blinded by its glare. I held up my hand against it.

"What's the matter?" said my neighbor. "Your father knew

what he did. Didn't have a problem admitting it at all. Blood on your hands. His hands. Blood on the whole family."

"That's enough," said a female voice, measured. "You're scaring him."

I know that voice, I thought, looking ahead of me for that familiar silhouette of shoulders, lavender-hued, the familiar brassy hair. The light made it impossible to see, although I had a terrible sense of movement all around me, toward me, scuttling across the floor. It was the guest lecturer; of course, she was part of it, too.

"Yes, Melissa," I heard the man at the lectern say, as if from a great distance. "She's right. Let's have them all off."

 Into the darkness swung the same sun-dappled clearing in the trees that I had just visited in my dream the night before.

Reclining on the marble tomb, propped up on one elbow, was Mr. Reinecke, as still as a sphinx, seeming again to be utterly without surprise at my sudden appearance. He flicked a lazy glance in my direction and then picked a piece of lint off his immaculate white sweater.

I've been here before, I thought, seen this before. But something about it is different.

"Coming up soon now, isn't it?" said Reinecke, with his customary uninterested air.

A brisk wind blew through the trees around us with a dry, papery rustle of the leaves.

"I don't know what you mean," I said.

Reinecke looked at me archly.

"Are you sure about that?" he said, a mocking curve to his mouth. "I think you know more than you pretend to."

I looked down. Did I? Then I was arrested by the sight of what I was holding in my right hand. I was no longer holding the briefcase—I was holding the whale-shaped paperweight from Professor Pindar's office.

"I'm afraid I can't stay," I said. I heard my own voice, but disembodied, as if the sound no longer corresponded to me.

"Yes, yes," said Reinecke with some weariness, as if he'd already heard this a hundred times. "You must go. But perhaps you might answer the phone, even so."

I opened my mouth to ask what he meant, but before I could I was made conscious of the faint sound of ringing, and Reinecke had produced from behind his person a telephone remarkably like the one in my office. It sat atop the white marble tomb, incongruous.

"It's for you," he said, and the sound of the telephone ringing grew louder and louder, until it drowned out everything else.

 "Hello?" I said. I was in my office and a considerable amount of time had passed. Through the telephone I could just barely hear the sound of light feminine breathing.

"Hello?" I said again. "Who's this?"

The breathing increased in tempo for a moment, and then the caller finally spoke.

"This is a friend," she said. It was a woman, as I'd thought, but she did not sound like either Linda in Professor Pindar's office or the guest lecturer.

"There's something I need to tell you," she said.

I looked out the window at the parking lot. Most of the cars had gone now, and the sky was awash in the soft dove-gray and golden light of dusk.

The prospect was unappealing, but I had no energy to resist. "What is it?"

"Can you meet me?"

I thought about that for a moment. I was so tired, and my meeting with the guest lecturer in the Arboretum had been so sunny and taxing.

"Oh, never mind," said the woman. "I saw you in the auditorium today."

"I'm sorry?"

"In the lecture hall—listen—I shouldn't be saying this, trust me, they will not appreciate it, but you shouldn't go back there—I can explain."

I tried to make sense of what she'd said.

"Go back where?" I asked. "Explain what?"

"It's for your own good—under no circumstances should you go to the hotel tonight. Really, you should never go there again."

The hotel, I thought. And: I have heard this voice before.

"What makes you think I'm going to the hotel? Why shouldn't I? Have we met before?"

There was a long pause, and then a silvery jingling noise, as if the caller was wearing a lot of bracelets.

"They're using you," she said, whispering now. "And yes, we have met. Once."

"At the—"

"Open house. Yes. It's Sharon," she said, in a whisper so soft I could barely hear it.

Of course, I thought, I could see her clearly now, coming down the path, the FOR SALE sign like a grounded white bird on the lawn.

"But *I* don't think you should have to pay for your father's mistake."

Her voice had taken on a shrill, self-righteous tone.

I drew in a breath, and pushed it out again through my teeth. Everyone seemed entitled to speak about my father today—first Professor Pindar and now Sharon.

"What mistake?" I asked, in a voice that was not quite my own. "Using me for what?"

"They want it to close," she said.

"Want what to close?"

"The hotel, of course," she said quietly. "It's a desecration."

This again, I thought. "A desecration of what exactly?"

Sharon made a chirping sound of disbelief.

"It's like making a hotel out of Auschwitz," she said, forgetting to whisper now. "The missions were—"

"Yes, yes, I know," I said, cutting her off. Really there was only so much of this one could take. "The missions were furnaces of death."

I hung up the phone, my heart ping-ponging in my chest, and when it slowed to a more reasonable speed I looked around. My foot was numb, and parts of my left knee felt perilously incorrect. The days when I could nap curled up like that had passed, that was for certain.

But was that what had happened? The love seat cushion was indeed imprinted with the outline of my head. Could that entire sequence of events—the meeting with Professor Pindar, the atrium, the lecture hall—have been part of my dream? That would, after all, be more believable than much of what had occurred.

But—the whale-shaped paperweight was sitting on top of a stack of papers on my desk. I picked it up and gave it a little shake. So it had all happened, implausible as it was. I looked over to where the leather briefcase was perched on the chair opposite, like a tiny, silent visitor. I slid it toward me across the desk and opened it.

I put the paperweight inside and closed the gold buckles with two crisp, final-sounding clicks. It was so much heavier now, I thought, as I rose to my feet with the briefcase at my side. Then came that strange feeling I'd had before in Professor Pindar's office, the one that took me far from the room, of the weight being familiar and somehow correct, as if I'd been meant to have it all along.

29 I'd made my move too quickly, I thought. I should have allowed myself more time to recuperate after the misunderstanding on the Alexandra Bridge, because it was that, and how I'd handled it, that had more or less caused the rupture with F, I could see now, almost thirty years later, as I nosed the car out of the medical school parking lot and onto Campus Drive.

Why *had* I called F from the hospital? On the one hand, it was true that at the time my circle of acquaintance had not been large, and it was F who had come to mind when the kindest nurse, after bringing me a blow dryer, a blanket, and a cup of hot coffee, had asked if there wasn't someone she could call who could come and drive me home.

It had been a mistake; I could see that now. Because if I was completely honest with myself, he had not just "come to mind," but something less savory: a part of me had hoped that the person who answered the telephone when the nurse called would be not F, but his wife or one of his children.

Because why should they be so oblivious? I thought. It did not seem fair that to them I did not exist at all.

Only by chance that I was alone and could come straight-away, F had written, in the note he left me at the breakfast table, the morning I'd gone to meet my father. *Only by chance.* Had he suspected? But, I thought, that was not relevant now;

it had all been so long ago. F's children most likely had children of their own now. There had been a time when I'd dreamt of it nearly every night, of the gray and swollen river rising up to meet me.

But honestly, I thought, anguished now, what an inconvenient time for all my thoughts to be pulled toward the past, and not just the general past, but to those particular weeks, the weeks I'd returned to with such alarming frequency in the last few days. I could not allow my thoughts to drift like this—I *would* not. I dragged them back to the task at hand; I chained them there by force.

Now I was coming along the edge of campus, and I saw that the fog had drawn in much farther than usual, completely obscuring the foothills in a wall of white. There was no real reason to think it, but I had the impression that I was driving to the Old Mission Hotel for the last time.

30

"Mr. Shriver," said the smooth-faced young man. He stood behind the reception desk, as doll-like and inscrutable as ever. Someone had replaced the vase of white lilies on the counter, and I became aware, as I had before, of their precise and not entirely pleasant scent. "We've been expecting you."

I gave him a long, slow, careful look, which he returned candidly.

"I see you've got your briefcase."

"Yes," I replied. I had the distinct impression that this was not the first time I had heard his voice that day.

"Were you there today?" I asked.

"Pardon?"

"At the lecture."

A silent pause went by, in which he held my gaze steadily.

"I'm sorry, sir, I don't know what you mean."

He reached into a drawer and retrieved a ring from which hung a key and a leather tag inscribed with the number 409. "I think you'll find the room very comfortable."

He opened his mouth again, as if to add something, but thought better of it. I took the key without comment and turned away, and had taken three steps toward the bar and the elevator when some extra sense caused me to turn back. The young man was watching me, and when our eyes met he treated me to a very beautiful smile, like a sunrise dawning on his lovely features. I had made the right choice, his expression seemed to say.

I crossed the lobby, passing the long bar. Its row of red candles looked as though they had just been lit, and yet the bar was deserted, and there was no sign of that surly bartender.

"Hey there," said a voice in the darkness. "There you are."

I turned and felt the briefcase bang painfully into my thigh as I swiveled in haste. It took my eyes a moment to adjust to the gloom.

"I think you've underestimated this place," said Mr. Reinecke. He was draped like a festive garland across one of the white, donut-shaped couches.

"I'm sorry?"

Beside him, on another of those distinctive couches, perched the little boy in old-fashioned clothing from my dream. He was sitting beside his mother, whose back was ramrod-straight.

"We'd prefer it if you came with us," he said.

"Just a minute," I said, with some difficulty. "What are you doing here?"

Then I heard another voice behind me.

"Sir?" It was the smooth-faced young man. I turned back toward the front desk, which, as suggested by the young man's current proximity to me, was unattended.

"Sorry, sir," he went on, and with a light touch on my elbow he steered me away from the donut-shaped couches. "I should have mentioned that the elevator is out of order."

And that was apparently true; ahead, I could see that a white paper sign had been taped over its buttons, the words written on it too small to read from this distance.

"Not to worry," said the young man calmly. "There is someone on the way."

I nodded, allowing him to guide me gently across the shiny floor, like a dance partner in some sedate medieval routine.

"There's no one in the lobby, Mr. Shriver," he said, the tone and volume of his voice unchanged. "You're in exactly the right place."

Now we had reached the door to the stairs, where the young man, still smiling, deposited me. I turned back to the lobby, feeling his eyes on me, tracking my gaze. Mr. Reinecke and the little boy had vanished—just as he had said, it was deserted.

Everything about the fourth floor was quiet; nothing could have looked more ordinary: it was the same thickly carpeted dark hallway I had been down before with the guest lecturer. Here I was, approaching the door to 409, key in hand. I paused. What if the room was already occupied? I raised my fist to knock.

Does this make sense? I asked myself. What was I planning to say, exactly, to the room's occupant?

But, I admonished myself, I had been paralyzed by indecision too many times before—now was the time for action, not more thinking. I knocked on the door three times: bright, sharp noises. Inside, I felt something—some presence—respond.

"Yes?" said a muffled female voice. "Come in."

"It's locked," I said, but when I looked down I saw that

I was wrong. In fact, the knob was turning smoothly in my hand.

The room was quiet and, at first glance, empty. There was the bed with its tight dark coverlet, the cabinet, the night table, and the desk. Everything was exactly like it had been before, only the time of day was different—then it had been night, and now it was merely drawing dusk, so that the setting sun tongued the hem of the curtain with an orangish light.

"In here," said the woman's voice, and I saw that the door to the bathroom was slightly ajar, and that the sound of the voice came from within, and that it was accompanied by the quiet splashing sounds a person makes while taking a bath.

"You're early," she said. It was difficult to say, muffled as her voice was, but I thought I detected a hint of irritation. "I'm not ready. But you can have a drink and wait."

A drink, I thought, and the words made a little echo in my mind. Then I saw that a bottle of gin, a bucket of ice, and two glasses were sitting on top of the cabinet, where they had not been previously. But before I could think with any meaningful result about that, a bright scrap of clothing caught my eye, and I leaned over the bed and saw that wedged between it and the wall was a lavender suit jacket, splayed out on the floor, its sleeves twisted as if it had been strangled. This turn of phrase struck me as funny: *as if it had been strangled.*

"Is someone dead?" Professor Pindar had asked. Yes! I thought. *It is the lavender suit jacket; it has been strangled!* I laughed, despite myself. And then I was interrupted by the woman in the bath—the guest lecturer, I reminded myself—because if her suit jacket was on the floor, then surely it was she.

"Hello?" she called from the bathroom. Now her voice was

unmistakably annoyed. "I couldn't understand anything you just said. If you didn't want a drink that's fine, but can you make yourself useful and get one for me?"

Of course it was the guest lecturer, I thought, as I moved away from the bed, from the suit jacket, back toward the desk. Because who else would it be? This was exactly the kind of bizarre and mysterious rendezvous she would prefer. Here was a person who was not content to arrange a meeting in the customary way, in a regular place—one's office, say, or a coffee shop. And yet, I could not quite say that she had arranged this rendezvous. I had come here of my own accord, for no other reason than the overwhelming sense that the answer to all my questions was here in this hotel.

"Yes, of course," I called in the direction of the bathroom, and then I smiled to myself, a small, private smile, because I had just set the briefcase down on top of the desk, its gold buckles gleaming in the waning light. I opened it and removed the paperweight.

Now I approached the cabinet and turned over one of the glasses. The briefcase! I thought. The suit jacket! Dusk creeping into night! Everything that held meaning was here in this room! How could I have stayed away so long?

Here was the red thread that had run through my whole existence. All that wasted time, I thought, as I tonged ice into a glass and poured gin over it; how lamentable, herding myself from one confusion to the next, when the answer had always been here in this hotel room. But! I scolded myself. Now is not the time for self-reproach! Holding the glass of gin in one hand and the whale-shaped paperweight in the other, I leaned my shoulder against the bathroom door and pushed it open.

I hadn't been inside the bathroom on my previous visit, so it would not quite make sense to say that something had changed. Still, as I stepped into the small, slightly steamy room, I had the distinct impression that I had crossed some more significant threshold, as if I had woken into a universe that was in every detail a copy of my own, but, in some essential way, different.

And this feeling, nebulous as it was, was somehow unrelated to the central unexpected feature of the bathroom, the main surprise it held, which was that the woman in the bath was not the guest lecturer. Despite the voice, which I'd thought I recognized, despite the lavender suit jacket, the woman in the bath, though she was also a blonde, also a big-boned woman, a nude woman who filled the small space amply, was not the guest lecturer; she was Kirstie.

She did not look up as I came in; she seemed to accept my entrance as an inevitable and not particularly interesting matter of course. Her hair, a truer, paler blond than that of the guest lecturer, had been piled on top of her head and secured with a blue plastic clip. At the other pole, a flushed and sturdy foot had surfaced—I could not bring myself to catalogue what lay between.

"Is that my drink?" she said abruptly. "You can set it there."

She indicated the lip of the tub, where a previous, now-empty glass sat, fogged with condensation.

"I think you may be under the wrong impression," she said at last, her voice unfriendly.

This was entirely possible, I thought; somewhere along the

line I had most certainly erred. There was no logical combination of events that should have resulted in this particular
scene. All I could manage, however, was a choked, "Oh?"

"I don't need your money," said Kirstie.

My money?

"Maybe that's how they did it when you were young, but
that wasn't what I meant at all. I may be a graduate student,
but I'm not exactly destitute."

My throat began to close around a dry and increasingly
useless tongue. Obviously there had been a case of mistaken
identity.

Now she was unwrapping a tiny bar of soap, liberating it
from its white paper jacket, and I had a flash of—

"No," she continued. "I told you because I was under the
impression that my pregnancy might interest you."

Her pregnancy, I thought, and before I could integrate this
new idea she went on:

"Yes, I know. You just wanted to deal with it. That's your
only mode, it seems. But you can go ahead and cancel that
appointment you made me at that Morgenthaler Clinic. It's
too far away, and I don't want an abortion from one of your
medical school cronies, thank you very much."

Now she rolled her eyes. "Excuse me, your *attending*."

Morgenthaler Clinic, I thought.

She had applied the soap to a washcloth and was soaping
her arms and shoulders vigorously, covering them in a layer of
white suds, and causing her breasts to dance a lunatic little jig.

After a long pause, she said resignedly, "Yes, I know. Linda
told me.

"No, of course not," she went on, "she was just being gossipy.

"Really, it doesn't bother me at all—I have tickets to go and see my parents. And I'm really not sure what you could do to help—whether you're in Jackson Hole or not. It will all be over by then.

"My parents? In Philadelphia. But don't you think the time for pretending to be interested in my family has passed?"

Still she did not look up, but her motions had an air of finality, she was giving the washcloth a thorough rinse. I supposed she was clean now, gleaming from head to toe.

Suddenly I found my voice.

"I don't think I'm supposed to be here," I said.

At my words a sudden sharp shift took place—a little crack in the vertebrae of the situation—and Kirstie turned to look at me for the first time.

"Well," she said, sneering. "Who knows what that's supposed to mean?"

I should try to explain, I thought. It's important to be precise.

"It's just that," I began—but already I could feel it slipping away from me.

"*It's just that*," said the woman in the bath, in a high and bleating voice that was meant to be an imitation of my own. She wrung the washcloth out with a violent twist, and it seemed to me, improbable as it was, that she was now the guest lecturer.

"It's just that," she began again, "you're not sure what you're doing here, and you'd like very much to, but you're not sure if . . . Is that right? Trust me, we know all about you and your *unique* challenges. We had hoped for someone with a little more oomph to them, someone a little more self-directed, but you were what we got. Still, we did have your general instability working for us. How lucky it was that you happened to show your hand in such a timely fashion. He assured us we were making the right choice."

She set the washcloth down beside her with a wet slap.

"Are you in a hurry, Mr. Shriver?" asked the guest lecturer.

I shook my head no.

"Good," she replied. "These things don't get arranged just like that, you know."

We were talking about something else now; that was clear. The tone of her voice had changed.

"See that candle?" she said, and for the first time I noticed a candle on the edge of the tub, a squat, peach-colored candle studded all over with seashells.

What an ugly candle, I thought. How was it that I hadn't noticed it before?

"Look at it," said the guest lecturer. "At the flame."

Obediently, I looked at the pale orange, dancing flame.

The lights in the room began to flicker and fade, until only the candle stayed lit. Then the bathwater, instead of behaving the way bathwater usually does, began to toss and pucker like a miniature sea. Tiny waves were breaking on the shore of the woman's white belly and lapping at the undersides of her breasts.

The flame wavered, grew slight and sputtered, and finally went out. The room was plunged into pitch-blackness.

———

Into the darkness, a new voice spoke.

"What are you doing in here?" it asked. This voice was a woman's, too. "You know I don't like it when you follow me around like a little dog."

I had, it seemed to me, some protest, but whatever it was it died on my lips; it dried up in my throat.

"Well," said the voice peevishly, and it seemed to me the voice was familiar to me, very much so, perhaps the most familiar voice of all. "Is there something you want to say? He won't like it, you know, if all evening you only stand around like a mute."

"Who . . ." I managed to say. "Who is coming?"

The voice clucked her tongue peevishly.

"Is that supposed to be funny? You know perfectly well it's your father."

My father, I thought, with sudden sharpness.

"My father?" I asked, in a voice as dry as sticks, as the wind rustling through dead grass. "How do you know my father?"

The woman in the bath was silent, and it seemed to me she was growing more and more like someone I knew by the second.

"Come over here," she said, her voice calm. "Come over here and I'll show you."

Does this make sense? I asked myself for the second time, as I crossed the room toward the bath and the woman in it. It seemed as though I were crossing the room for eons, as though I had to cross the whole horizon to get there. When I reached the edge of the bath, I realized that the lights in the room must have restored themselves at some point, because I could see the woman clearly, though I tried not to stare down at her naked body: the flat breasts with their dark nipples, the thatch of hair that sprang between her legs.

"Kneel on the floor," she said, and when I hesitated, she said, "Go on."

Don't, I told myself, lose the thread—but already it was spooling away from me, I sank to my knees beside the edge of the bathtub and found myself looking into my mother's eyes.

I did not see her lift her hand—did I ever? Only a bright blackness that stung me on the temple.

"Now," she said.

How changeable this woman is, I thought. Nothing is fixed.

"What was that question you asked? Do you need to ask that question again?"

"No," I whispered.

"No is right," she said. "Now come and rub your mother's head."

Thoughts small and large flooded my brain. Stick to one thing, I told myself, as I knelt behind the woman in the bath and began to stroke her thin brown hair. I drew one thumb across her forehead and then the other. Two fingers, I thought, and the thought ballooned in me and then vanished.

"You know," said my mother in a dreamy voice, her eyes closed. "It is really a shame that he won't come and stay longer. Wouldn't you like that? To have a real father, like all your little friends?"

I nodded, though I knew she couldn't see me.

"I know I would like that," she said. "Of course, you don't know how exhausting it is, raising a child on your own.

"You know," she went on, splashing the water languidly

with her hands, "I know you might want to pester him when he comes, but you might try being a little less attention-seeking, do you know what I mean? He travels a long time to get here, and he wants a boy, not a little dog following him around and breathing down his neck."

I nodded again, behind her back.

"Now that I think of it," she said, shifting a little from side to side, "that might have been the problem, last time. Because he was meant to stay the whole weekend, wasn't he?"

She crossed her arms over her belly, and above them her breasts lay like two collapsed balloons.

"And I had so much planned, so that was a shame. We won't let that happen again, will we? You will try to be more self-sufficient?"

There was a thing, deep inside me, and this conversation had piqued its interest, and while my mother had been talking and I'd been rubbing her temples, it had scrabbled up bit by bit, so that now it had reached the base of my skull.

"Young man?" said my mother. "Did you hear what I said?"

There was a sound as the water splashed. She shifted around. I heard her laugh, a nervous, ragged sound.

"What is that?" she said. "What's that you have in your hand?"

"Oh, this?" I said. "This is just something I picked up earlier."

Because of course it would have been impossible to explain about Professor Pindar and his harpoon, and how he was descended from New England whalers. Even though I feared gravely for my ability to keep the right thoughts afloat, I knew that those things were not relevant here, in this time. Because I could recognize this as one of the many evenings (though perhaps, I thought, there had only really been a handful, each one blazing out of my memory as brightly as Christmas) when my father had been due for a visit at my mother's house and had failed to appear.

Now I brought the paperweight down. *One!* And again. *Two!* Something gave beneath it, a bright noise.

Because (*Three!*) I thought, as I brought the paperweight down again to meet the noise. What is a face, in the end? What is a face, but a layer of skin over bone? Because, I thought, as I raised it up and brought it down, this face has changed so much, in such a short time—surely, and again it came up and down, like a hammer at a fair, this is not the way a face should be. Surely, I thought, a face should not be so changeable. Surely, I thought, and another thought crept up beneath it like a worm: *This face has run its course.*

I had paused for a breath, to wipe sweat from my brow, to allow the other thought to come up to the surface and bloom, when I saw that at the other end of the tub two long, gray feet were groping for purchase, slipping and sliding on the white porcelain.

That is not good, I thought, and I brought the paperweight down again, and this time I held it there with all my strength, until the gray feet shuddered and stopped. Through the water, a red tide rode toward them. And then the thought broke over me, immense, and I knew that this was what had eluded me for so long. I am two fingers! I thought. I am the steeple. I am, I thought, and it was the last thought that came to me before the room shuddered and went black—I am the Death that lives within the walls, these walls that have such a long and storied history of Death.

When I opened my eyes, the room was dark again, almost black. Eventually, I stood up; I switched on the light. I surveyed the scene.

In the tub was an arrangement that seemed hardly to belong to this current reality. Now that she was dead, the woman in the tub had changed again. She was no longer my mother, that was certain, but whether she was Kirstie or the guest lecturer again, I couldn't tell. I felt spent, exhausted like I hadn't been in years. How much nicer would it be, I thought, if I were home, sitting at my dining room table, watching the fog roll in from the sea. I would almost certainly have made my sandwich by now, and I would be without obligation, with nothing to do but watch the fog come creeping up the lawn to reach through the pines like long white fingers.

Some time should be spent here, I thought, even so, and I took one last look around. This, I thought as I turned, looking at everything with care, was just the right amount of death. I would not make the mistakes *they* had made. I would not be too heavy-handed. Someone coming after me, someone in the midst of their own investigation—they would understand; they would not be left like I had been, my nose buried in my father's coats, harassed by the bleating of the real estate agent. I had left things just right. But just in case, I thought, twirling on my feet, paperweight in hand, coming out of the bathroom—just in case, because you could never be sure of the caliber of other people, I would leave them a little clue. It was a shame, undoubtedly, to stain the lovely suede of the briefcase with blood, but it could not be helped. Then I buckled the bright gold buckles and slid it under the desk.

31 In the dark I heard Gerry Van Gelder's deep voice say, "Is that you?"

The porch light switched on, a white globe in the night.

"It's me," I said.

I heard the sound of bolts unlocking, and then the door opened to reveal a frowning, enrobed Gerry Van Gelder, peering through glasses. He looked at me and said, "Do you know what time it is?"

Really, Gerry, I thought. These people and their obsession with time. If only I could have shown him how it felt—life, death—but I held back; I refrained. To be inside the house first would be best.

"I don't," I said. "But it must be late."

"Yes," said Gerry. "It *is* late."

"Who is that?" came Ann's voice from the darkened hall. "Oh gosh, it's you," she said.

Gerry looked at me, his arms crossed.

"Could I come in?" I said. "I didn't know where else to go."

"Something wrong with your house?" said Gerry.

"Oh, let him in, Gerry," said Ann. "He'll let us know soon enough."

Gerry looked at me, expressionless, and then held the door open so I could pass.

"Thank you," I said, as he re-bolted the door. "I must be very late."

"Late for what?" Gerry asked.

"Okay, Gerry," said Ann, appearing in the hallway in her own bathrobe and white socks. "That's enough.

"Come on," she said to me. "I'll make you a plate."

She motioned for me to follow her into the kitchen, where she opened the refrigerator and peered inside.

"I made chicken," she said, frowning into the light. "We could heat it up, but it might actually be better cold . . ." She trailed off, because she was looking at me more closely now, under the bright kitchen light. She drew her breath in with a hiss.

"Where have you been?"

Somewhere close by a telephone was ringing.

"Are you kidding?" said Gerry under his breath. "Who is calling at this time of night?"

Ann was still looking at me with the same concerned expression, but when I gave her no encouragement she went back to the refrigerator and opened the door. I lost interest in the little scene for a time, and when I returned there was a plate of chicken and roasted potatoes on the counter in front of me, and Gerry was saying, "Yes, thank you," and hanging up the phone.

"Who was it?" Ann asked.

The look on Gerry's face was strange. He was moving slowly now, back toward the kitchen, as if he wanted to figure something out before arriving. He cut a dumpy and unappealing figure in his bathrobe, his long legs pale and spindly beneath its hem.

"Well," he said, hesitating. He looked at me, an unreadable expression on his face. Then he said to Ann, "Stephanie isn't coming back until tomorrow, is she?"

"No," said Ann. "What? Who was that on the phone?"

He did not respond immediately, and I waited, without much interest, for him to go on.

"Were you?" he said nonsensically, turning abruptly to me. "Kirstie Johanssen," he said suddenly. "Isn't she the one . . . who knew your father?"

Ann was looking at me, too, now, and when I did not respond she said, "Yes, I think so," and then to Gerry, incredulous, "That was who was calling? Kirstie Johanssen?"

"No," he said. "No, no."

He was looking at the countertop with uncharacteristic intensity. "That was someone else. Kirstie Johanssen is missing."

Ann closed the refrigerator door. "Missing?" she repeated. "What does that mean, missing?"

Gerry did not answer, or if he did I didn't hear him—I was regarding Ann contemplatively, as if really seeing her for the first time in a long while. She has aged badly, I thought. But how exactly, it was more difficult to say. Like an old shoe that you have had for many years, after a certain point it becomes difficult to tell how it might look to other people.

They were both looking at me now. Ann, who had just poured a glass of water, put it down slowly in front of me, like she had forgotten what it was.

"What was that?" she said.

I was silent, at first, and then I said, "I didn't say anything."

"But of course you did," said Ann. Her brow furrowed, and then she laughed as if despite herself. "You said I looked like an old shoe."

I opened my mouth to protest, but no words came out—I could not explain it.

They were even closer now, Gerry especially, until both their faces, curiously blank, were mere feet from mine, and I felt myself inspected. Not only that, I felt suspicion in their gaze. Was it possible? I thought. Could they know already?

"Nothing!" I burst out, and swept my arm up to emphasize my point—but in doing so I knocked the glass Ann had just set down off the counter, and next I heard it crash into a million pieces on the floor.

"Silly me," I said, quietly and to myself, looking down from my perch to the shards twinkling up at me.

Glass, I thought. Life, two fingers, and then the room went sideways, and because of the proximity of the shards to my open eye, I deduced that I was now lying on the floor.

32 We have one dream, and then each year we make it a little smaller, all the while saying to ourselves that it's to be expected, after all. This little success will do. Then this smaller one. So I will not have professional success, but I will have a good home life; I will marry well. And then it is the next year, then it is several years later, I will not have professional success, if I have not found some willing applicant for love, I will seek pleasure in solitude. And so on and so forth.

I find I am brimful of thoughts like these. Gems of wisdom, each one riding like a wave on the back of another wave. Here I am in a narrow bed, low to the floor, in an unfamiliar room, sparsely furnished, with a single high window in the corner through which the morning light falls in fat bars across the thin brown blanket. On the wall is a framed picture of blue cartoon rabbits roller-skating. *Not* an interior decorating scheme that inspires much confidence, but when it comes to my thoughts, I am in an orchard and the fruit is ripe, I wander through the trees in a perfect light.

Stirring, I feel an unfamiliar warm patch against my thigh, and reaching down I am delighted to feel the soft fur and cold ears of what is unmistakably a cat. This is that black cat, the most obese of the three Van Gelder cats, I think, stroking it.

Ann and Gerry, I remember. This is their house. This must be their spare room. Here is the glass of water Ann left on the nightstand.

Through the walls of the house I hear the click of the front door opening, and Ann's voice says, "Come in." Early for a visitor, I think; judging by the light it could not be later than six or seven in the morning. Now here is Gerry's voice, in its low register, joining in. Footsteps in the hall.

The door opens, and the light in the room has changed. It could be that it's actually the next day, or the next. Keeping track of time has proven more difficult than it had initially seemed. Here is an old man wearing a well-cut gray coat, who sits down in a chair which has suddenly materialized beside my bed.

"How do you do?" I say, because it seems only polite because of where he is sitting; we are very close together.

He's looking at me intently but does not respond. His eyes have a hooded, turtle-like quality to them, and very softly, as if they are very far away indeed, I hear a soft tinkle of bells. You know this man, the bells say. But I can't place him.

"I'm handcuffed to the bed," I say suddenly, and as I say it, I realize that it's true. It's my right hand, and the other side is fastened to my bedpost. For a moment I am less certain that this is Ann and Gerry's house, but I push this thought aside.

The old man's eyes flick to the handcuffs, but still he doesn't speak.

"But that makes sense," I say, trying my best to fill the silence. "I killed someone."

For a second the man's face experiences a little stutter,

and freezes. But then he recovers, recovers himself totally, and raises one eyebrow as if to say, *Oh, really? Whom?*

"That's an interesting question," I reply, as if he had asked it out loud. "It's sort of hard to say. Could have been one of three people."

But that's not quite right. And then a new, unrelated thought pushes to the surface: Could it be, as I am in Ann and Gerry's house, that this old man is Ann's father?

It is true that he looks nothing like he did at Thanksgiving. This man, the one sitting in the chair in front of me, seems more robust, but it is not outside the realm of possibility.

"I've known Ann and Gerry for years, a long time," I say ingratiatingly, hoping this will get a response.

Nothing.

"We were neighbors, in graduate student housing," I say. "It's funny how the mind works, I can barely remember that apartment now."

It was true. I can barely remember it now, the apartment where they'd been my neighbors. I had had the mistaken impression that my father would meet me there when I arrived. Why, I don't know; I can see now that it was an illogical expectation. I can't remember now who it was who handed over the keys, who walked me through those unmemorable rooms, but it was not my father.

In fact, I saw him only once, I'm fairly certain, after my arrival at the university and before his death. It was early in the morning, the first truly cold morning of autumn, and the grass on the Oval was silvered with frost. I was walking towards the main quad, wishing I had worn a thicker jacket, when I saw my father standing beside the Burghers of Calais, whose figures, I saw, had been wrapped head-to-toe in burlap and rope, a bizarre sight.

Neither he nor I made any gesture, though I am certain he saw me. Our eyes met. Then the moment passed and he turned back to his companions, a well-dressed man and woman whom he seemed to be leading on a tour.

ACKNOWLEDGMENTS

My most sincere thanks to Rebecca Curtis, my first, best writing teacher. Thank you to Paul LaFarge, Victor LaValle, and Ben Marcus for their guidance.

Thank you to my editors, Eric Chinski and Julia Ringo, and my agent, Claudia Ballard, for their time and dedication to this book.

A debt of inspiration is owed to David E. Stannard and his book *American Holocaust: The Conquest of the New World*.

For their support and encouragement, my thanks to Zeynep Kayhan, Yvonne Woon, Medaya Ocher, Andrew Eisenman, Ezra Koenig, Marya Spence, Meghan Sutherland, Willing Davidson, Ahna O'Reilly, and Eugene Kotlyarenko.

Thanks to the Ucross Foundation of Ucross, Wyoming, the Ragdale Foundation, and Vermont Studio Center.

Last, thanks to Evan Small and Lev Wilder Small for their patience.

A Note About the Author

Sara Davis, the daughter of two Stanford immunologists, grew up in Palo Alto, California, and received her bachelor's degree and MFA at Columbia University. She has taught creative writing in New York City and Detroit. She lives in Shanghai, China. *The Scapegoat* is her first book.